FORCED EXODUS

Pandemic Book Two

CHRISTINE KERSEY

SAPPHIRE
CREEK
PRESS

The characters and events portrayed in this book are fictitious. Any similarity to real persons, living or dead, is coincidental and not intended by the author.

Forced Exodus (Pandemic Book Two)

Cover by Novak Illustration

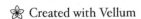 Created with Vellum

BOOKS BY CHRISTINE KERSEY

Pandemic Series

Pandemic: The Beginning (Pandemic Book One)

Forced Exodus (Pandemic Book Two)

Parallel World

Dare to Resist (Parallel World Book One)

Dare to Endure (Parallel World Book Two)

Dare to Defy (Parallel World Book Three)

Dare to Oppose (Parallel World Book Four)

Dare to Prevail (Parallel World Book Five)

Witness Series

Witness (Witness, Book 1)

Retribution (Witness, Book 2)

Ashley's Billionaire

Snowed in with the Billionaire

Assistant to the Billionaire

Trouble with the Billionaire

Ever After with the Billionaire

Billionaires Find Love

The Protective Billionaire

The Missing Billionaire

Don't Look Back (Lily's Story, Book 2)

Love At Last (Lily's Story, Book 3)

Life Imperfect (Lily's Story, Book 4)

Over You Series

Over You

Second Chances (sequel to Over You)

Standalone Suspense

Suspicions

No Way Out

CHAPTER 1

Matt

MATT BRONSON'S gaze slid from door to door to door as he drove down his street. The same red X was painted on the vast majority of his neighbors' houses. It was the mark of death, meaning there was one or more bodies inside. A corpse dead from the bird flu. Nearly his entire neighborhood was dead, as was most of the world from what he'd been able to gather before the grid had gone down.

And the stench of rotting corpses. It was a smell he didn't think he'd ever get out of his nostrils.

It had been a little more than two weeks since the pandemic had exploded and he and his family had hunkered down, but since then their world had gone sideways. Even so, they were still alive, which was more than could be said for the vast majority of the population.

Frowning deeply, he forced his attention back to the road as he drove his truck, which was pulling their fifth-wheel RV, out of their neighborhood. He and his family had been through so much, and now they were at the beginning of a brand new journey. A mix of hope and trepidation washed over him, and he wondered if Jessica felt the same. He glanced over at her. She was staring out of the passenger window with her chin resting on her curled fist.

She turned to him with a melancholy smile. "Do you think we'll ever come back?"

They'd loved living in their house for the previous two years and the idea that they would never see it again brought on a whole mix of feelings—sadness, anger, frustration. Slowly shaking his head, he lifted his shoulders in a shrug. "I don't know." He didn't want to point out that thanks to the neighborhood cooperative, their house had burned to the ground, so even if they did come back, they wouldn't have a place to live. Besides, in all reality they'd never return. They were going to start fresh in California.

Softly sighing, Jessica went back to staring out the window.

Letting his gaze slide to the rearview mirror, Matt checked on Kayla, Brooke, and Dylan in the back seat of his truck. All three were wide awake and completely silent, their eyes scanning the neighborhood.

"Nobody's around," Dylan said.

"It's barely six o'clock in the morning," Kayla said with a yawn.

The kids had hardly left the house since the pandemic had broken out. Except Brooke. She'd had to venture to their house on her own after both of her parents had died of the bird flu. Well, she and her dog Cleo. Matt looked over his shoulder to see what the German shepherd was doing, but he couldn't see her. "How's Cleo?"

"She's sleeping on the floor," Brooke said.

"Sorry it's so tight back there," he said with a grimace. "One of you can sit up here between mom and me if you want."

None of the kids volunteered to sit between the adults. Was that because they preferred to be parent-free in the back or because they were nervous about being closer to the potential line of fire in the front?

That thought led Matt to cut his gaze sharply to the houses they were passing. Which houses had the gang members moved in to? He had no idea. All he knew was that at least twenty dangerous gang members had taken up residence in their neighborhood, which was why they'd decided to bug out rather than find another house to move in to. And now they were headed to California with Derrick, Jeff and Emily, and Chris and his family.

Matt's eyes went to Derrick's truck, which led their little caravan. Derrick, an ex-military man—as Jeff and Chris were —was watching for trouble ahead. All four of their vehicles had walkie talkies so they could alert each other before they found themselves in trouble. At least, that was the plan.

They rolled through the stop sign that led out of the neighborhood. With no traffic and no police, there was no reason to slow their momentum. Several minutes later they passed the Home Depot where Matt and Derrick had "shopped" a week earlier, then they approached State Street. They were almost to the I-15 on-ramp, the Interstate they would take on their journey to Central California.

3

The walkie squawked on the console between the seats and then Derrick's voice came over the line. "Roadblock ahead. Approach with caution. Over."

Matt's heart pounded as adrenaline surged. They'd barely left their neighborhood and already they were running into potential trouble.

"I see the roadblock," Jessica said, her gaze riveted to the road ahead.

"Yeah." Matt touched the .45 on his right hip to reassure himself that it was easily accessible. "Me too."

"Can't see around the RV," Jeff said over the walkie. "What's the roadblock look like? Over."

Matt glanced in his sideview mirror. He couldn't see Jeff's truck behind him—he was too close to the back of Matt's RV. But he could see Jeff's small utility trailer. He could also see Chris's SUV, which brought up the rear.

"Vehicles blocking the approach to I-15," Derrick said. "SUV's and trucks. Men with guns standing behind the vehicles. No way around them." A brief pause. "Turn right on State Street. We'll try for the next on-ramp. Over."

Derrick's truck hung a right. Matt's gaze shot to the men who watched them from their protected positions behind their trucks. One man spoke into a walkie of his own.

Matt began the turn onto State Street, and as he focused on getting his rig around the corner smoothly, he said, "Jess, tell the guys that one of the men at the roadblock just spoke to someone on a walkie."

She looked at him with fear in her eyes but did as he asked.

"Copy that," Derrick said in reply.

"Dad," Kayla asked with urgency as she leaned forward, "what's going to happen? Are we going to be okay?"

Torn between wanting to reassure her and wanting her to know the truth, he said, "We're doing our best." Then, as the RV straightened and they began heading north on State Street, he threw her a smile. "Derrick, Jeff, and Chris are the best. I'm sure we'll be fine." He glanced at Jessica, who smiled at him as if to say *I know you're trying to reassure her. Thank you.*

Love for the woman he'd grown to appreciate all the more over the previous two weeks swept over him. He reached out and took her hand in his, squeezing gently.

He checked his right sideview mirror and saw Jeff, then Chris, turning onto State Street behind him. His eyes went to the road in front of him. Only one car length separated him from Derrick's truck. Not a lot, but they wanted to stay close.

They approached the turnoff to Costco. Remembering how insane it had been when he'd stocked up two weeks earlier, Matt shifted his gaze to the left. He couldn't see the Costco parking lot from where he was, but he was fairly certain it was empty.

Nearly a mile before they would reach the next on-ramp. Normally that wasn't far, but with the unknown stretching out in front of them, the distance seemed enormous. A lot could happen in a mile.

Matt picked up the walkie. "What can you see up ahead? Over." Matt let his gaze wander over the cars at the car dealership on the left as he waited for Derrick's reply.

"Looks clear from here," Derrick said, "but I can't see what's on a Hundred and Sixth. Over."

Matt frowned. They would have to turn left at 10600 Street to get on I-15.

5

"Hang back," Derrick said. "I'll scout ahead. Over."

"Copy that," Matt said. Jeff and Chris each said, "Copy."

They were about a hundred yards from their turn when Matt brought the RV to a stop.

Moments later Derrick's voice came over the walkie. "We have a problem. Over."

CHAPTER 2

Jessica

AT DERRICK'S WORDS, Jessica's heart began thumping painfully against her ribs. Gaze shooting in all directions, she tried to find the problem, but she couldn't see anything. Derrick had driven to the point where they needed to turn left. Were men blocking that entrance to I-15 as well?

The thought of confronting men with guns terrified her. Could they be gang members? The ones who were killing whomever stood in their way? Sickened at the thought, she tried to keep her negative thoughts from spiraling out of control.

Then she thought about the long journey ahead. If they were already facing a problem, how could they possibly travel the seven hundred miles to the San Joaquin Valley without traversing all kinds of danger? Would they even make it?

Glancing at her children, she couldn't stop herself from imagining how she would feel if anything happened to them.

It would destroy her.

Hot tears pricked the backs of her eyes.

Wanting to hide her tears, she turned toward her window.

"What's going on?" Dylan asked from the backseat.

"I don't know," Matt said.

Chris's voice came over the walkie. "Status? Over."

"Armed men approaching," Derrick said. "Wait one."

Jessica squinted into the distance. Then she saw them. Two men with guns drawn and surgical masks covering their mouths and noses were striding up to Derrick's truck. Derrick's hands were sticking out of his window. When the men reached the truck, one of them pointed his gun right at Derrick as the other lifted the handle on the driver's side door before pulling it open. Derrick stepped out with his hands in the air. He also wore a face mask. One of the men turned Derrick around before patting him down.

"What are they going to do?" Jessica asked, gaze glued to the scene a hundred yards in front of her. When Matt didn't answer, she turned to him. "Matt?"

Expression grim, he shifted his gaze to her. "I don't know."

They turned their attention back to Derrick.

A third man approached and said something to the other two. They holstered their guns and the newcomer nodded to Derrick. The men and Derrick seemed relaxed as they stood there talking. After several minutes Derrick motioned Matt forward.

Jessica wasn't sure she wanted to get any closer, but she also didn't want to leave Derrick on his own. They needed him. Alive and healthy.

With fear compressing her chest, she braced herself for what might come next.

Matt put the truck in gear, and they lurched forward.

"What are you doing?" Jeff asked over the walkie.

Matt picked up the walkie. "Derrick wants us to join him."

"Copy that," Jeff said. "On your six."

They slowly moved forward, stopping fifteen feet behind Derrick's truck. Derrick and the men he was talking to looked their way. Matt put on his surgical face mask, then reached for his door before turning to Jessica. "You going to wait in the car?"

She'd planned on it, but as she thought about it, maybe a woman's gentle touch could help. Gathering her nerve, she shook her head. "No. I'm coming."

"I wanna come," Dylan said from behind them.

Though her reflex was to tell him no, it would do him good to see how they handled this. At least she hoped so. Things looked calm and friendly enough that she didn't fear for him.

Matt looked at her with raised eyebrows.

"Okay," she said to Dylan. "Put your face mask on."

Grinning, he undid his seatbelt and opened his door. Jessica and Matt got out as well. Jessica looked behind them. Jeff and Chris were approaching. The five of them—all masked—walked toward Derrick and the three men.

Derrick turned to them and nodded, which served to calm Jessica completely. Everything was going to be all right.

"Ran into an old friend," Derrick said, glancing at the man standing in front of him. "This is Ben Atkinson." Derrick introduced Jessica and the others.

Ben greeted them. "I'd shake your hand, but..." He raised his eyebrows.

"What's with the roadblock?" Jeff asked as he crossed his arms over his powerful chest. One of his guns was clearly visible on his hip. Jessica noticed Ben's eyes going to it briefly before he met Jeff's stare. "Trying to keep people from leaving town?"

All eyes turned to Ben to hear his explanation.

"Actually," he said with raised eyebrows, "we're trying to keep out the people who don't live here. I presume you've heard about some of the gangs that've been wreaking havoc."

Jeff dropped his hands to his hips as he nodded. "Okay. I can appreciate that." Then he squinted. "But *you've* got to appreciate that when people like us see something like that," he gestured in the direction of the roadblock, "it makes us nervous." He cocked his head. "When I get nervous, people tend to get hurt." He glanced at Derrick, Matt, and Chris before turning his sharp gaze on Ben. "Sometimes killed."

After what had happened at the barn—Jeff interrogating the two gang members who had moved in to their neighborhood before he killed them—she knew he was deadly serious. She was just glad Jeff was on *their* side.

"Didn't mean to make you nervous, bro," Ben said with a chuckle. "Certainly don't want anyone getting hurt or killed."

Jeff didn't respond, just continued staring.

Ben ignored Jeff and turned to Derrick, who looked like he was working to hold back a laugh.

Derrick looked at Ben. "So, we're good?"

Ben's eyes crinkled like he was smiling. The tension eased. "Yeah. Good to see you."

"Likewise." Derrick paused a beat. "You take care."

Ben nodded once, then he and his men drew away, leaving their little group to have a brief powwow.

CHAPTER 3

Matt

DERRICK TUGGED down his face mask. Everyone followed suit.

"Ben says they've turned away a number of travelers. People who were pretty desperate. People who are now out there." He motioned in the general direction of I-15. "Sounds like it's gonna be rough out there." He grimaced. "Which is kind of what I expected."

That wasn't something Matt wanted to hear, but he wasn't surprised.

Derrick gestured toward the RV, concern in his eyes. "That rig's gonna be a prime target. But with the solar panels, water tank, and other amenities, it's a huge asset to us." He looked at each person in turn. "How far are you willing to go to keep it?"

Matt glanced at Jessica and Dylan. The moment Matt had agreed to go on this trip, he'd known having the RV would be both a blessing and a curse. He dearly hoped they would still have it when they reached their destination, but the lives of Jessica and the kids were the most important thing. He compressed his lips. "It's not worth losing a life over but I'm not going to give it up easily either."

Derrick nodded. "Agreed." He looked at the others and everyone nodded. "Okay. We're on the same page." Then he smirked at Jeff. "You already know your utility trailer will be a target."

Rolling his eyes, Jeff chuckled. "Yeah."

Derrick laughed. "Just so we're all clear on what's what."

"Is the RV or Jeff's trailer worth taking a life over?" Jessica asked.

They all turned to her, but no one answered. Matt didn't want to have to kill anyone—there had been enough killing already. Besides, his RV wasn't worth a person's life. "No," he finally said.

Derrick held up a hand. "Hold on." All eyes swiveled to him. "It's impossible to say exactly what situations we'll run into, which makes it impossible to state anything with certainty." He grimaced. "We're going to have to figure things out on the fly."

Matt couldn't disagree, but he wanted clarification. "Are you saying there might be an instance where you would kill over losing our supplies?"

"If losing those supplies meant endangering our lives, then yeah. Absolutely."

Okay. He could see the reasoning behind Derrick's statement. He just hoped that wouldn't be something they would face.

As they walked back to their vehicles, Jessica spoke

quietly. "I'm nervous, Matt. About this trip. About what could happen."

He put an arm around her shoulders and tugged her against him. "We need to have faith that we'll all be okay. Besides, we have an awesome team." He chuckled. "What could be safer than traveling with Derrick, Jeff, and Chris?"

She tossed him a sideways glance. "Not traveling at all."

That got his attention. They reached the truck. Dylan got in, but Matt faced Jessica. "Are you having second thoughts? About leaving?"

Shaking her head, she sighed. "Staying would be just as dangerous. Maybe more with those gangs living in our neighborhood. It's just..." She looked at the pavement before meeting his eyes. "I worry. You know that."

He kissed her before pulling her into his arms. "Yes. I do know that." He worried too, but he had to shove that down and focus on each moment as it came. He drew away and smiled at her. "Let's not get ahead of ourselves, okay? Instead of thinking about what *could* happen, let's concentrate on what *is* happening."

Softly smiling, she said, "How do you always know the right thing to say?"

Chuckling, he said, "I'm awesome like that."

She hugged him. "Yes you are."

They got back in the truck, and moments later they lumbered forward with Derrick leading the way. When they passed Ben and his crew—who had moved their cars enough to allow their caravan to pass—Matt lifted his hand in greeting. Ben gave him a chin lift. Moments later they drove down the on-ramp and entered I-15. The last time Matt had been on the ten-lane interstate, he'd been coming home from work at

Jessica's behest. Traffic had been lighter than normal, but nothing like now. Now, the only cars moving on the road were the ones in their group. A car was parked haphazardly on the shoulder here and there, but no one was near those cars.

With no traffic, they drove in the northbound lanes unimpeded, although Derrick kept their speed to about forty-five miles an hour. Matt was glad. It would conserve their fuel as well as give them the agility to go around unexpected objects in the road. Chris and Jeff stayed behind Matt, spreading out a bit in the adjoining lanes.

Matt looked ahead and saw nothing but clear roads. It seemed unlikely that anyone would expend energy blocking this road. Why would they bother with so little traffic?

"Look at that," Jessica murmured, pointing to the southbound lanes.

Matt shifted his eyes to the lanes going the other direction. That's when he saw them. Ten people were walking south, most of them with something covering their mouths and noses, a few of them pushing shopping carts overflowing with all of their worldly possessions.

The pedestrians stopped and stared at Matt and his group as they passed.

"Where do you think they're going?" Brooke asked. She was sitting beside the window that had the best view.

"Somewhere warmer?" Jessica asked.

Matt thought of Ben's comment that they'd stopped a lot of desperate people from entering the area. Would these people be the next group Ben would come into contact with?

"They'll probably go wherever they can find food," he said, which reminded him of how blessed they were. Although now that they had twelve people in their group, plus Cleo, their food stores would dwindle more quickly.

They'd traveled less than three miles when the walkie squawked and Derrick's voice came over the line.

"Pedestrians up ahead. Slowing to pass them. Over."

Matt focused on the road up ahead and was able to make out a small group of people walking right down the middle of the Interstate. "I see them."

"Where?" Dylan said from behind him, leaning halfway into the front seat.

"Put your seatbelt on," Jessica said.

"How come? There's, like, no cars on the road."

Matt glanced at Jessica. She looked at Dylan with narrowed eyes and a deep frown.

"Really?" she said. "You think just because there's no traffic that Dad won't have to slam on the brakes?"

Dylan huffed a sigh, but Matt heard his seatbelt click into place.

Derrick's brake lights came on, so Matt braked as well. Following Derrick's lead, Matt carefully swerved to the left to go around the people walking in the center lane.

"Hey!" one man yelled as he threw a rock at their truck. "Help us out. Give us some food."

CHAPTER 4

Jessica

A ROCK HIT Jessica's door. She let out a small scream. Sweeping her gaze over the people they were slowly passing, she saw two men, two women, and three school-aged children. Clothes dirty and torn in places, hair matted, dragging their feet as they staggered along the asphalt, they looked like they'd been on the move for a while.

"Help us," one of the women cried out. "Please!"

Jessica bit her lip, then looked at Matt, who frowned.

"Can we help them?" Kayla asked, her eyes beseeching.

Jessica wanted to help them too, but in all reality, if they helped every person they came across, they would quickly run out of food and then they'd be in the same situation. They had to make it to their destination—the San Joaquin Valley in California where Emily's aunt and uncle had some land where they could settle and make a home.

"I'm sorry, sweetie," Matt said, "we have twelve mouths of our own to feed. We really don't have extra."

He glanced at Jessica, she assumed to see if she would argue with him, but she smiled and placed her hand on his, adding, "We need to stay focused on our mission."

The people walking faded into the distance.

"Our mission?" Kayla asked.

"I know what it is," Dylan said.

Turning her attention to Dylan, Jessica smiled. "What?"

He grinned. "To get to that place in California."

"That's right."

Kayla pursed her lips. "I still don't see why we couldn't give those people a little bit of food."

"Tell you what," Matt said, "next group of people we see, we'll give them some food."

Surprised that he was willing to do that, Jessica looked at him with raised eyebrows.

"What?" he said with a chuckle.

Reaching out and stroking his cheek, she said, "I just love you."

He took her hand and kissed it. "I love you too."

It didn't take long before the next group of pedestrians came into view—two men and three women. All five of them waved their hands as Matt and Jessica's convoy approached.

Jessica looked at the group, then said, "I know we can only help a few people. Let's wait until we see a group with children."

Matt nodded. "I agree."

They went on, soon exiting onto I-215 on-ramp. I-215 was the connecting freeway to get them to I-80, which would take them all the way to California.

Derrick's voice came over the walkie. "Blind curve ahead. Approaching with caution. Over."

Matt and the others acknowledged his message.

On edge as they got closer to the curve, Jessica fixed her gaze on the road. She'd driven this way dozens of times, always speeding around this bend to merge with northbound I-215 and never thinking twice about it. But now, what if there was a roadblock? A pile-up of cars? What if they were ambushed?

She hated this—the danger, the unknown. It was so outside of anything she'd experienced before, and knowing there wasn't a darn thing she could do about it beyond endure and deal with it didn't help.

They went around the bend smoothly without incident, merging with the non-existent traffic.

Exhaling the breath she hadn't realized she'd been holding, Jessica knew by the time they reached their destination, all of her hair would be gray.

The walkie squawked. "Slowing down. People up ahead. Over."

Jessica looked at Matt, suddenly unsure if she wanted to stop and help people after all. The fear she'd just experienced made her nervous about stopping.

"Look!" Kayla said as she pointed out the window. "There's kids."

"Looks like a family," Matt said with a glance in Jessica's direction, a question in his voice.

One man, two women, and two young teenagers—a boy and a girl—pulled a full wagon behind them. All five of them turned and looked at the approaching vehicles, but they didn't break their stride and they didn't try to wave them down.

Jessica looked at Matt and nodded. He picked up the walkie. "We're going to stop. Over." He set the walkie down.

"Not advised," Derrick shot back.

Jessica picked up the walkie. "Just this once, over."

To her pleasure—and surprise—Derrick came to a stop about twenty feet past the group.

Matt braked to a stop ten feet in front of the people. The walkers looked alarmed. Wanting to assure them that they were there to help, Jessica stuck her head out the window and shouted, "Hello!" in her friendliest voice.

One of the women, who looked like she was in her forties, waved and smiled wanly, like she had the weight of the world on her shoulders. "Hi."

"Can I talk to you for a minute?" Jessica asked.

The woman glanced at her companions, who were eyeing all four vehicles with suspicion, then she nodded. "Okay."

Jessica tugged on the door release. As her door began to open, Matt grabbed her arm.

"Wait," he said.

She turned to him. "What's wrong?"

He frowned. "Don't get out."

Jessica looked at the people. The woman she'd spoken to was striding toward the truck, walking right up to her window. Alarmed at the woman's swift approach, Jessica closed her door and yanked on her face mask.

"Do you have any food?" the woman asked through the window.

Jessica turned and looked at Matt with raised eyebrows.

"Here, Mom," Kayla said, handing her a granola bar and a bottle of water.

Jessica turned to Kayla with eyebrows furrowed. That food was supposed to have been Kayla's breakfast. Had she been holding on to it so she could give it away?

Love for her daughter swept over her.

"Please?" the woman asked, her voice pleading.

With a tender look at Kayla, Jessica took the meager meal and held it out to the woman standing just outside her window.

The woman looked at the food with a frown before glancing at the rest of her group. Turning back to Jessica, she snatched the food from her hands. "Got anything else? This won't go far." Her voice had gone from pleading to annoyed. "I know you've gotta have a whole lot in your rig." She gestured toward the RV with her thumb.

The woman was right, but Jessica wasn't about to get out of the truck to go into the RV, and when the woman sneered and said, "Come on. Don't be selfish," all feelings of compassion fled.

"I'm sorry. That's all I have to give."

Now the woman's eyes narrowed before her lips pressed into a slash. "You're lying."

CHAPTER 5

Matt

MATT DIDN'T LIKE the surly tone the woman was taking. He shifted into gear and took his foot off the brake. "Time to go."

Jessica nodded.

The walkie squawked and Jeff said, "Move! Now!"

Not taking the time to figure out why Jeff's voice sounded so urgent, Matt hit the gas and the RV jerked into motion. Derrick was already driving, his truck more agile without an RV tethered to it.

"Mom!" Dylan shouted. He was sitting behind Jessica, next to the window. "Get down!"

On instinct, Matt put his hand on Jessica's upper back and shoved her so that she would bend forward. A bullet whizzed past her and nearly hit him, lodging in his headrest.

The kids screamed.

Heart thundering in his chest, Matt clenched his jaw as he took his hand from Jessica's back, his focus on getting his family away from the flying bullets. She straightened.

The sound of several more gunshots rang out. He braced himself to be hit, but nothing happened. He looked at Jessica, his eyes raking over her as he searched for injury. "You okay?"

She nodded.

"Everyone else okay?" he called out.

Each of the kids said yes, but their voices were shaky.

Matt's eyes drifted to the right sideview mirror. That's when he saw the man lying on the ground and the rest of his group kneeling beside him.

The walkie squawked. Jeff spoke. "Threat has been neutralized. Over."

"Copy," Derrick and Chris said.

Stunned with how quickly things had gone south, but grateful that the other men had his back despite his bad decision to stop in the first place, he picked up the walkie and muttered, "Copy." He set the walkie down and shifted his gaze to Jessica, who looked shell-shocked. "No more stopping, okay?"

Mutely, she nodded.

Keeping his left hand on the steering wheel, he reached over and placed his right hand on one of Jessica's. She closed her eyes as her chin fell to her chest, then her shoulders silently shook.

Furious with those people, he gritted his teeth. They'd stopped to help them and they'd shot at his wife. But now the man was dead. He didn't feel any remorse about that whatsoever.

"It's okay, Mom," Dylan said from the back seat as he reached forward and patted Jessica's shoulder.

"Yeah," Kayla said, "you were only trying to help. How were we supposed to know they'd turn on us?"

Matt could hear Jessica drawing in a shaky breath.

"They shot at us." She turned to Matt with tear-filled eyes. "What if they'd hit one of the kids?"

"Let's not do what ifs, okay? We're all fine and we've learned a lesson."

She looked in the sideview mirror on her side of the truck, then swiveled to Matt. "What if they'd hurt one of the others? Chris and Amy have little ones in their car." Her eyebrows bunched. "It would be all my fault."

He looked at her with raised eyebrows.

A tiny smile lifted her lips. "Right. No what ifs."

Not wanting to squelch that part of her that wanted to care for others, he said, "You know, there may come a time when we can actually help someone. Someone who will be grateful."

Her eyes brightened. "Do you think so?"

Actually, he had no idea if that would ever happen, but he couldn't resist the hope in her eyes. "Yeah." Besides, it was possible.

She smiled, then leaned back in her seat.

They drove several miles in silence.

"I think Cleo needs to go to the bathroom," Brooke said.

Trying not to sigh, Matt picked up the walkie. "Cleo needs a potty break. Over."

"Copy," Derrick said with a chuckle. "Road looks clear. We'll stop here, but make it quick. Over."

"Jacob needs to go too," Chris said over the walkie, referring to his six-year-old son.

"I'm glad Cleo's not the only one," Brooke said with a laugh, relieving some of the tension.

Matt smiled. A few moments later the RV stopped. In an

overabundance of caution, Matt got out first. Derrick was out of his truck as well. Matt scanned the freeway. No threats visible. He opened the rear door. Brooke hopped out with Cleo.

"Go potty, girl," Brooke said as she held Cleo's leash, but Cleo seemed more interested in sniffing the asphalt than taking care of business.

Come on, Matt thought as he continued surveying the area. Finally, Cleo was done. Matt looked toward Chris's SUV. Chris gave the thumbs up. Breathing a sigh of relief, Matt made sure Brooke and Cleo were safely inside before he got in. Derrick pulled forward and Matt followed.

Traveling with children and a dog would make things a little more challenging, but that was just the way it was. They would all adjust. They'd have to.

They passed the Valley Fair Mall. The Maverick Center was coming up on the right. Matt looked toward it, thinking of the good times he'd spent there watching hockey games with Dylan.

"Sniper! Sniper! Sniper!" Derrick yelled just before a bullet slammed into the grill of Matt's truck.

Matt didn't know where the shot had come from, which made it impossible to know how to avoid the next one.

"On the overpass!" Jeff called out.

Matt's gaze shot to the overpass they were rapidly approaching. Two men were pointing rifles right at them. "Everyone down!"

His family cried out in fear, but all he could do was make sure they weren't hit again. With the RV on his back, Matt had no agility to swerve, but he did his best, cutting to the right to avoid the snipers' bullets.

Derrick and Chris cut and swerved, but with his small utility trailer, Jeff was in a similar situation as Matt.

"Look!" Dylan shouted.

Matt couldn't turn to see what he was pointing at. "What? What is it?"

"Emily! She's shooting back!"

Matt's gaze jerked to his sideview mirror. Sure enough, Emily was pointing a rifle out of the passenger window, shooting at the snipers. Taking advantage of the cover, Matt surged forward, hurtling under the overpass and racing away from it as fast as he could. The others did the same, and soon they were out of range of the men on the overpass.

Matt kept an eye on his gauges to watch for any indication that his radiator had been hit. Looked okay. He would check for damage when they reached a place that felt safe to stop.

Moments later another overpass came into view.

"Oh no," Jessica moaned.

Matt picked up the walkie. "Do you see anyone on this overpass? Over."

After a brief hesitation, Derrick answered. "No, but let's hurry past it. Over."

"Copy."

They drove underneath it without incident. When they were safely past, Matt exhaled in relief.

On high alert, they continued north, and before long they made the turn west toward I-80.

CHAPTER 6

Derrick

REVIEWING the incident with the pedestrians, Derrick compressed his lips and shook his head. He should never have allowed Matt to stop. He'd known better. Sure, people might be grateful for help at first, but in the end the people they stopped to help would do what they had to do to survive. Even if that meant killing the person trying to help them.

As he drove west on I-80, his eyes constantly scanning for danger, he allowed a grim smile to blossom on his lips. Good thing Jeff had been back there to take care of the problem when the man had opened fire. Derrick didn't want to kill anyone—none of them did. But if they were shot at, he would return fire. And he was an extremely good shot. So was Jeff. Emily wasn't bad either. He didn't know Chris's shooting skills, and Matt was TBD.

Shaking his head, he couldn't hold back a chuckle. Despite Matt's penchant to act first and think later, Derrick liked the guy. His family too. They were good people. He especially approved of them taking Brooke into their family like she was one of their own. He'd known her father—a good man. Derrick knew her father would be pleased that his daughter was with the Bronsons now.

The West Temple overpass was coming up. Still shocked that they'd been shot at while driving on a road he'd driven dozens of times before, Derrick scanned the overpass for snipers. No one was in sight.

He thought about the snipers he knew. If they'd been the ones shooting at them, the situation would have turned out very differently. Good thing the snipers they'd faced hadn't been very good shots.

He picked up the walkie. "Overpass looks clear. Over."

"Copy," came back.

They passed beneath several more overpasses without incident and Derrick began to feel more comfortable.

The 201 overpass, which merged with I-80, was two hundred yards ahead. He thought he saw a flash of something, but he wasn't certain. He wasn't going to take a chance. "Be on alert. Over," he said into the walkie before setting it on the console between the seats.

The others acknowledged the warning.

When all four vehicles had passed beneath the 201 over-pass with nothing happening, he exhaled. Then movement on the on-ramp caught his eye. He looked to the right, eyes widening at a sight he'd never expected to see stateside—a pickup truck with a machine gun mounted to the roof and a man standing in the bed of the truck. In battle, a setup like that was called a technical. The man swiveled the gun in Derrick's direction as the truck raced down the on-ramp.

Snatching the walkie from the console, Derrick jammed

his finger into the Talk button. "Technical on the right!" He tossed the walkie onto the passenger seat while at the same time crushing the gas pedal and charging forward.

Gunfire poured from the machine gun, aimed right at him. Wanting to draw the gunfire away from the other vehicles in his group, Derrick sped up. The technical sped up too. It was working, but were others waiting to attack? He dearly hoped not because he couldn't do anything to stop them from shooting at his group.

The others are capable. It's not all on me.

The reminder helped him focus on his own problem— being shot at by a determined enemy. The technical was closing in on his tail and he had nowhere to go. He yanked his sidearm out of his holster, powered down the passenger window, then swerved to the left and slowed down enough to let the technical catch up with him.

Bullets battered his truck. Ignoring that, he slammed on the brakes, letting the technical sail past him. Then he stomped on the gas, bolting forward, then braked, varying his speed, making himself harder to hit. Keeping a sharp eye on the machine gunner, when the man ran out of ammo, Derrick took advantage of the lull, surging forward. With his gun held in his outstretched right hand, he aimed in the direction of his open passenger window. He aligned with the gunner, then slowed his speed to match that of the truck before pulling the trigger in quick succession until the man was hit, tumbling out of the bed of the pickup truck and onto the asphalt of I-80.

Next, Derrick turned his attention to the driver, coming up alongside him. The man was no idiot. His gun was pointed out his window toward Derrick. Quickly backing off, after a moment Derrick sped up and twisted his steering wheel to the right, clipping the bumper of the enemy truck. To Derrick's satisfaction, the truck spun out of control, slamming into the guardrail before coming to a stop.

Derrick slowed, his eyes on the driver. Blood poured down the man's forehead and a deflated airbag sagged from the steering wheel. But the man stayed in his seat, his eyes open.

These men had attacked without provocation. If Derrick didn't do something to stop them, the next travelers probably wouldn't survive. With a grimace, Derrick turned his truck around and approached the truck with caution. Fifty feet away, and with the technical on the left side of his truck, Derrick watched the man. Could Derrick shoot him in cold blood on the chance—the very high chance—that he would attack others? Not sure, Derrick stared at the man as his truck crept closer.

The man glared back. Derrick had his gun in his right hand but kept it in his lap. When it came down to it, he didn't want to kill someone who was helpless and injured. But what about the next driver that came along, innocent and unsuspecting? What if they had children with them? What if Derrick could prevent a tragedy?

Undecided, he drifted closer.

Five feet from the truck, Derrick lifted his gun but kept it held low. Four feet, three feet, two feet. His gun was just below his window. He looked directly into the man's eyes. They were filled with hatred.

Heart pounding with indecision, all he had to do was raise his gun a few inches and it would all be over. But he hated the idea of shooting a man in cold blood. What if the man had a family of his own? Then again, he and his buddy had come out of nowhere to attack Derrick and his friends unprovoked.

The man shifted in his seat. Sun glinted off metal. A gun came into view, tipping in Derrick's direction. Not hesitating a moment, Derrick lifted his gun the two inches necessary to clear his window frame and pulled the trigger. The man fell back, a hole in his forehead.

Shoulders sagging as he exhaled, Derrick stopped and shifted his truck into park. He hadn't wanted to do it, but the man had drawn on him, giving him no choice. It had been the right thing—the *only* thing—to do.

After verifying that no other enemy vehicles were around, he climbed out of his truck. Scanning the interior of the truck, he saw the gun the man had held plus two additional weapons and boxes of ammo.

"What did you find?" Jeff asked as he trotted up to Derrick.

Derrick smiled grimly, then looked at Emily, Chris, and Matt as they joined him at the truck.

"A few weapons to add to our arsenal." Derrick chin-pointed to the bed of the truck. "That machine gun might come in handy as well."

Chris grinned. "Absolutely." He jumped into the bed of the truck and unmounted the machine gun. Jeff joined him, gathering up the extra ammo.

Once they'd stowed the newly acquired weapons and ammo, both Derrick and Matt assessed their trucks for any engine or tire damage from the bullets that had hit them. Both trucks looked okay.

The group gathered in a loose huddle around the hood of

Derrick's truck where he spread out a map of the area. Amy, Chris's wife, as well as Jessica and her kids, joined them

"It's over a hundred miles before we reach Wendover," Derrick said as he tapped a finger on the town just over the Utah border. "Most of those miles will be on the Salt Flats, which means..." He raised his eyebrows and turned to Dylan, testing the kid to see if he knew the answer.

Wide-eyed, Dylan said, "Nowhere to hide?"

Pleased he'd answered correctly, Derrick grinned. "That's right for the most part. Even so," he looked at each of the adults, "we have to assume there will be some sort of danger, so we need to stay on high alert at all times."

"Do you want me take point for a while?" Jeff asked.

After the gunfight he'd just been in, Derrick was ready for a break. He nodded. "Yeah, that would be great." He turned back to the map and pointed to a tiny dot. "We'll reach this rest stop in about an hour, depending on our speed. Let's stop there and regroup."

Heads nodded all around. They got into their respective vehicles, and with Jeff leading, they fell into line: Jeff, Matt, Chris, with Derrick taking up the rear.

CHAPTER 7

Jessica

"DERRICK'S A BADASS," Dylan said with obvious admiration.

Holding back a smile, Jessica glanced at Matt, who gave her a sideways look.

"What do you mean?" Kayla asked. "Emily shot at those snipers when no one else did. I think *she's* a badass."

"I want to be like that," Brooke said, her voice soft like she didn't want anyone but Kayla to hear. But Jessica had heard, and she felt the same way. *She* wanted to be like that too—able to take care of herself and her family instead of being scared and nervous all the time.

Shifting in her seat, she faced the kids. "We can all be as brave as Emily and Derrick."

Matt placed his hand on hers. She turned to him with a smile. One side of his mouth quirked up, then he said, "You already are."

Eyebrows pulling together, she stared at him. "Why do you say that?"

"When that bullet flew past you, you didn't freak out."

"No, but I cried."

Smiling softly, he put both hands on the steering wheel, glancing at her as he spoke. "Only because you regretted stopping. Not out of fear."

He was right. Her confidence grew. "Huh."

He laughed.

The drive across the Salt Flats was one of the most boring drives, and usually Jessica dozed for the two-hours it took to cross it. But that was before. Now, she couldn't fall asleep if she wanted to. Instead, her eyes were constantly scanning, scanning, scanning. She hadn't seen any people walking on I-80, but it had only been fifteen minutes.

A flash of metal caught her eye. It was a car. Traveling east. There were two lanes in each direction with a wide area in between. Sage brush and flat white salty ground lay in the space. No concrete barriers. The median could be easily traversed.

Was the driver of the car in the opposing lane friend or enemy? Dangerous or harmless? Was he alone? Were other cars not far behind? Would the driver cross into the westbound lanes and cause trouble? Shoot at them?

Two weeks earlier that thought would have been ludicrous. Now, it was a distinct possibility. Especially after being shot at several times that day already.

"Car approaching in the eastbound lane," Jeff said over the walkie. "Over."

"Copy," the others said.

Jessica's heart thudded dully in her chest. Then the words she'd said to her children less than fifteen minutes earlier filled her mind. *We can all be as brave as Emily and Derrick.* This was her chance to prove it, to show her children that they could all be brave. She straightened her shoulders and touched the gun at her hip.

Moments later the car passed them by. No shooting.

Exhaling audibly, Jessica began to relax. Not everyone was out to get them or to take what they had.

They drove on, passing a few people walking on the shoulder, and eventually they cautiously followed Jeff into the rest stop parking lot.

No other cars were there and no people were visible, but there were plenty of places to hide.

When their truck came to a stop, Jessica reached for her door.

"Hang on," Matt said, stopping her.

She turned to look at him.

"We need to clear the place before you and the kids get out."

"I can help," Dylan said from the back seat.

Jessica was about to tell him no when Matt said, "That's a great idea."

Scowling at him, Jessica was about to argue when she had a better idea. "The girls and I should help too."

Matt's eyebrows shot up and Jessica wanted to take back what she'd said. Then Kayla leaned forward and said, "Count me in."

Half hoping Matt would tell Kayla no, but also knowing this was something they all had to learn how to do, Jessica gazed at him, waiting to see what he would say.

His lips compressed as his eyes went to each of them.

Finally, he said, "Yeah. Okay." Without another word, he opened his door and hopped out.

"Yes!" Dylan said with a note of triumph.

Tossing Dylan and the girls an encouraging smile, Jessica was pleased to see a look of grim determination on the faces of both Kayla and Brooke.

"We *are* brave, Mom," Kayla said.

Feeling her courage growing, Jessica nodded. "Yes, we are."

They all got out. Moments later they stood with the rest of their group. Jessica's gaze went to Amy and her young children. She hadn't had a chance to talk to Chris's wife, but the poor woman looked exhausted. Traveling with young children under normal circumstances wasn't easy. Being under constant threat would make it ten times harder.

"We need to clear the building and the surrounding area," Derrick said. He made assignments, leaving out Jessica and her kids.

"Hang on," Matt said.

Derrick turned to him with a question on his face. "What is it?"

"Jessica and the kids need to learn how to clear a building."

Pleased that Matt was speaking up for them, Jessica slipped her hand into his. He squeezed gently.

Derrick nodded. "Yeah. The more trained people in our group, the less burden it is on the rest of us."

Jessica hadn't thought of it that way, but she definitely wanted to carry her own weight. And she knew that the more she was able to do, the more her confidence would grow. Same for her children.

"Okay," Derrick said, "Dylan's with me, Kayla with Jeff,

Brooke and Cleo with Chris, Jessica with Matt. Emily, stay with Amy and her kids. This shouldn't take long." He told them which area to clear. She and Matt were assigned to clear the men's restroom. "Meet back here after you clear your assigned area."

They all nodded.

Glad Derrick had assigned her to stay with Matt, as they approached the building, she noticed a sign that said *Watch for snakes and scorpions*. Arching an eyebrow, she looked at Matt, who chuckled.

They walked toward the glass-fronted building that held both the men's and women's bathrooms. Matt stopped outside the door and took out his gun. He told her to do the same. Eyes widening, Jessica felt her heart skip a beat. This was suddenly all too real. What if she had to shoot someone?

Then she remembered how terrifying it had been when that bullet had flown past her hours earlier. She couldn't allow someone to threaten her or her family. Besides, most likely no one was in there.

She pulled the 9mm from her waist.

Matt watched her. "Is it ready to fire?"

"I don't know." She hated her lack of expertise.

"Rack the slide."

She did. He showed her how to tell if the safety was off. It was.

Smiling grimly, he nodded. "Now it's ready." His smile vanished. "Stay behind me." Jeff and Kayla, who were assigned to clear the women's bathroom, were right behind them. Jessica looked at Kayla, who had a gun in her hands and a look of grim determination on her young face.

The sight sent a thrum of sadness and pride through

Jessica. It was better that Kayla knew how to defend herself than be afraid of guns.

Matt peered through the glass door. After a moment, he pulled it open and stepped through, his gun held low and ready. Jessica stayed close to him.

She heard Jeff and Kayla enter behind them, but a moment later they went toward the women's restroom whereas she and Matt went toward the men's restroom.

Matt paused outside the door. He looked at her with raised eyebrows. Heart rate increasing, she nodded.

Leading with his gun, Matt stepped into the men's room. Jessica studied his every move. She knew he wasn't an expert, but Derrick had trained him. That was good enough for her.

Light filtered in from the high windows along the wall.

As Jessica crossed the threshold, she realized this was the first time she'd been inside a men's room. A slight odor of urine permeated the air and the place was definitely less clean than women's restrooms usually were.

Pushing aside those pointless thoughts, she watched Matt as he cleared the first stall, and when he motioned for her to do the other one, she inhaled sharply—then immediately regretted it, wrinkling her nose at the smell.

Matt chuckled and shook his head.

She tossed him a smile before turning her focus back to the stall she was about to clear. It seemed likely that it was empty, which made it easier to push the door open all the way. No one was inside.

Feeling a burst of pride that she'd done this instead of waiting in the truck, frightened and helpless, Jessica beamed. "All clear."

Matt grinned and tugged her into his arms. "Mrs. Bronson, you are looking mighty sexy right now."

Giggling, Jessica snuggled against his chest. At that moment, they weren't in the beginning of the apocalypse. Instead, they were a couple in love enjoying one another's company.

Then a shot rang out.

CHAPTER 8

Matt

AT THE SOUND of a gunshot from somewhere outside, Matt's first instinct was to pull Jessica closer. Then he remembered that his children were out there.

Another gunshot rang out, then another and another.

"The kids!" Jessica shouted as she sprang away from him, eyes wild with fear. "We need to get the kids!"

He grabbed her hand and raced out of the bathroom. Jeff was already in the foyer.

"Where's Kayla?" Jessica whisper-screamed.

Jeff gestured toward the women's restroom with his head. "Told her to wait in there." He squinted at Jessica. "You should wait with her."

Matt agreed. He didn't want her or Kayla—or any of their kids—anywhere near flying bullets. He shifted his eyes to Jessica. Her eyebrows furrowed like she was reluctant to leave Dylan and Brooke outside where the shooting was taking place while she hid inside.

"Kayla needs you," he said.

She sighed, then nodded before turning and heading toward the women's restroom. Once she was out of sight, Matt followed Jeff's lead, pressing against the wall as he crept toward the sheets of glass that fronted the entrance to the bathroom area.

No one was visible in their line of sight. Instead, directly in front of the building sat Matt and Jessica's RV and the others' vehicles.

Jeff took point and Matt followed, stepping through the doorway and into the sunshine, then paused. The gunfire was coming from their left. Creeping along the concrete block wall, they worked their way to the corner of the building. That's when they saw two men shooting from the covered picnic area, using the brick supports as cover. The men popped their heads out, taking potshots at whoever was on the other side of the bathroom building.

Worried that Dylan or Brooke could be hit, Matt wanted to neutralize this threat immediately, but they didn't have a clear shot.

"Go around to the other side?" Matt asked Jeff, who was studying the men in the distance.

Jeff shook his head. "No. We have a clearer shot from this angle." He grinned at Matt. "And they don't know we're here."

"How do you want to play it?" Matt was ready to start shooting, but he wasn't the expert here. Not yet anyway. With the way things were going, he would be soon. Not something he relished learning.

Jeff told Matt his plan. It was risky, but Matt didn't have a better idea.

Jeff looked at Matt, took a breath, then nodded once. Matt pointed his gun toward the men and began shooting. Jeff bolted out from behind the wall and raced toward the picnic area. Keeping his eyes on the men he was shooting at, Matt kept track of Jeff with his peripheral vision. In less than five seconds, Jeff reached the picnic area. Not wanting to hit Jeff, Matt stopped shooting. So did whoever had been shooting at the men from the other side of the bathroom building, presumably for the same reason.

The enemy took advantage of the lull and shot toward Matt. Matt pressed himself against the brick wall, staying out of range. Bullets slammed into the wall around the corner from him and shards of brick flew past him. Several more shots rang out and then all was silent.

"Jeff!" Emily screamed.

Oh no! Matt jerked his head around the corner of the building and looked toward the picnic area. Three men lay on the ground—the two shooters and Jeff. Emily was flat-out running toward Jeff with Derrick right on her heels.

Matt took off too, his heart in his throat.

Emily fell to her knees beside Jeff. Derrick was there half a second later.

When Matt reached them, he saw a bloom of red on Jeff's left shoulder, but Jeff's eyes were open. He was alive.

The two men, on the other hand, weren't moving. Matt looked at Derrick, who touched each man's neck. Derrick shook his head. They were dead.

"We need to help him," Emily said, her voice frantic.

"I have a first aid kit," Matt said before dashing to the RV, getting it, and running back to their group, who now included everyone but Jessica and Kayla. He opened the kit and handed it to Emily. He wanted to get Jessica and Kayla—he didn't like the idea of them being on their own right now. What if there were other gunmen around?

CHAPTER 9

Jessica

THE CONSTANT GUNFIRE set Jessica's nerves on edge. Who was shooting? Was anyone hurt? Then the shooting stopped. Heart throbbing with fear of the unknown, Jessica looked at Kayla as they stood in the middle of the women's restroom. She needed to find out what was happening, but she was also scared to leave the relative safety of the restroom.

"I need to go to the bathroom," Kayla whispered.

Torn between wanting to hustle outside and wanting to stay where they were, Jessica bit her lip. Then again, it would only take a minute to take care of business. Besides, she needed to go too. "Okay, but let's hurry."

Kayla went into one stall while Jessica went into the one beside hers.

The moment Jessica locked the door to her stall, the sound of footsteps entering the bathroom echoed. Was that Matt coming to get them? Why wasn't he calling out to let them know it was him? Or maybe it was Emily.

The footsteps came closer, stopping nearby. Foreboding swept over Jessica. She moved back, pressing her body against the corner of the stall, her eyes riveted to the tiny gap around the door.

"I know you're in there."

The voice belonged to a woman. She sounded upset and angry.

Who was it? Was she alone? Was she dangerous? Who was she talking to?

Kayla was in the stall next to Jessica's, but she was completely silent. Obviously, she didn't want the woman to know she was there. And with the wall between the stalls reaching the floor, Jessica couldn't silently communicate with Kayla.

A brisk knock on Jessica's stall door startled her. She let out an audible gasp.

"I knew it! You're in there!"

Heart battering her ribs, Jessica could see the woman's feet—heavy boots with a broken lace—just outside her door. With no idea what to do, she took comfort in the fact that the woman probably didn't know Kayla was in the other stall.

"Open the door!" Pounding with both fists accompanied the words.

Slapping a hand over her mouth to smother a scream, Jessica's eyes widened.

Matt! Where's Matt?

All at once Jessica remembered she had a gun at her back. Hands shaking, she pulled the 9mm out of her waistband, glanced at it to make sure the safety was off, then pointed it at the door. "What do you want?"

"Oh. She speaks."

"You have the wrong person."

A maniacal laugh filled the air. "Are you with the people outside? The ones who killed my man?"

Her gaze shot in all directions. What exactly had happened out there?

More pounding. "Are you?!"

Startled, Jessica almost dropped the gun but managed to keep it in her control. She gripped it more tightly, steadily pointing it at the door. "Leave now."

"Or what?" The tone was taunting. "I saw you. With those people. And then you came in here with one of the men. He came out but you didn't. So don't try to lie to me."

Swallowing over the knot in her throat, Jessica gathered her courage. She had to protect Kayla, had to protect herself. She inhaled, then said, "This is your one and only warning. I'm going to count to three. If you're still in this bathroom when I get to three, we're going to have a problem." She didn't want to flat-out tell the woman she had a gun. What if the woman had a gun of her own pointed at the door right now? What if she shot first? Trapped in the tiny stall, Jessica would have no way to dodge flying bullets.

The woman didn't respond, but Jessica could see her feet planted right in front of the stall door.

"One," Jessica said, working hard to keep her voice from shaking. She paused a beat. "Two."

The feet shuffled away from Jessica's stall.

"Maybe you're the wrong one," the woman said, her voice still very close.

Jessica nodded. She was the wrong one. She hadn't done anything. Not yet.

"Maybe it's the girl I want."

Kayla! She meant Kayla! The woman knew Kayla was in the other stall! Jessica had to do something and do it now.

Licking her lips, Jessica crouched down and tilted her head to see exactly where the woman was. She barely managed to see that the woman was standing in front of the neighboring stall, the one Kayla was in.

A soft knock sounded on Kayla's stall, like the woman was trying to be gentle. "Knock, knock," she sang out.

"Leave me alone!" Kayla shouted.

Still crouching, Jessica squeezed her eyes closed for a moment. Now the woman knew for sure that Kayla was in there.

The woman laughed, but this time it sounded dark and menacing. "Ollie ollie oxen free."

"I'm not coming out," Kayla said, her tone laced with determination.

"Oh no?"

"No."

"I don't think you understand," the woman taunted. "You *have* to come out. It's only fair." She paused. "A life for a life. Your life for my man's."

Jessica's heart slammed harder against her ribs. This woman wanted to kill Kayla? For something she had nothing to do with? As long as Jessica had breath in her body, she would never allow anyone to hurt her baby girl. Falling to her knees, she got close to the filthy ground and lowered her gun, poking her gun out of the stall and toward the woman's booted feet. She didn't want to do this. She really, really didn't, but she couldn't let the woman hurt Kayla. Besides, this shot wouldn't kill her. Only disable her.

Forcing her hands to remain steady, she slid her finger

until it was touching the trigger. Her eyelids fluttered closed as she considered what she was about to do. Maybe she could reason with the woman, explain that she and Kayla had nothing to do with what had happened outside.

The walls of the stalls began to shake violently as the woman screamed and pounded, demanding that Kayla *open the door right now!*

Kayla screamed in terror and Jessica's eyes snapped open. With a grimace of reluctance, she squeezed the trigger.

BOOM!

The sound of the blast echoed off the walls of the bathroom, nearly deafening Jessica, but she was so focused on what she was doing that she hardly noticed.

The woman screamed in pain, falling to the ground as a gun clattered to the tile floor, skittering under another stall.

Jessica twisted the lock on her stall and yanked the door open, her eyes snapping to the woman before scanning the restroom for other attackers. They were alone.

Holding her gun in the low ready position, she stepped out of the stall, then pointed her gun at the woman.

The woman moaned and held on to her foot, her gaze jabbing at Jessica. "You shot me!"

Forcing away the guilt that swept over her, Jessica stared at the woman. "Move out of the way." She used her gun to indicate that the woman should slide away from Kayla's stall.

"Or what? Are you going to shoot me again?"

It didn't seem as if the woman posed a threat now, so of course Jessica wouldn't shoot her. But she wasn't about to admit that. She just wanted Kayla to be able to safely come out. "Ignore me and find out."

Eyes wild with pain and fear, the woman used her good

51

foot to propel herself to the other side of the bathroom. A trail of blood from her wounded foot smeared across the floor.

Keeping her eyes on the woman, Jessica called, "Come out, baby. It's safe."

A moment later the lock on the stall turned and the door opened a few inches. Kayla's face appeared in the gap, her mouth hanging open and her gaze bouncing between Jessica and the woman on the floor. "Mom?"

Holding her gun with her right hand and keeping it pointed at the woman, Jessica held out her left arm to Kayla, who rushed into her mother's embrace. "It's okay," Jessica murmured, which was laughable. Nothing in their world was anywhere near okay.

CHAPTER 10

Matt

ABOUT TO LEAVE Jeff and the others so he could get Jessica and Kayla, when the unmistakable sound of a gunshot filled the air, Matt bolted toward the building that housed the restroom, his focus solely on getting to his wife and daughter.

Cautiously entering the building, he swept the foyer with his gaze, his gun at the ready. He thought about his family being taken hostage in the barn in his old neighborhood only the night before and the tactic he and the other men had used to rescue them. As much as he wanted to burst into the bathroom to save them, he had to be smart. It wouldn't do anyone any good if he got himself killed.

A tap on his shoulder made him jump. Glancing behind him, he was relieved to see Derrick there to back him up.

"Which room are they in?" Derrick murmured.

"Should be the ladies' room."

Offering a quick nod, Derrick gestured for Matt to take point. Clenching his jaw in determination, Matt moved forward, his body tense, his ears straining to hear anything that would give him a clue as to what was happening.

Moments later he crossed the threshold into the women's restroom and peered around the corner. A woman he'd never seen before lay on the floor, her foot bleeding. But to his everlasting gratitude, Jessica and Kayla stood over the woman, appearing whole and healthy.

"Dad!" Kayla said, stumbling toward him as tears filled her eyes. He wrapped her in his arms. Jessica stayed where she was, her gun pointed at the injured woman.

"What happened?" Derrick asked.

Jessica told them what had transpired, ending with, "She claims you guys killed the rest of her group, but I don't know if that's true."

"It is," the woman said, her voice wavering between pain and fury. "It was me and Evan and Todd. Thanks to you it's just me now."

Derrick frowned. "We didn't want any trouble, but your friends shot at us unprovoked."

The woman scowled.

"Her gun's in there," Jessica said, pointing to a stall.

Derrick retrieved it, tucking it into his waistband.

"Jeff's been shot," Matt said.

Jessica's eyebrows rose as she lowered the gun. "What? How badly is he hurt?"

"Not sure yet." They needed to get back to their group. Especially since they didn't know for sure if there were others in this woman's group. Others who were a threat. "We need to go."

"What about me?" the woman cried, her face screwed up in obvious pain.

Derrick quickly searched the woman, then knelt beside her. Gently removing her boot and sock, he examined the wound. "It's only a flesh wound." He turned to Matt. "Can you get a first aid kit?"

Matt didn't like the idea of leaving Jessica and Kayla, but he had complete confidence in Derrick's ability to keep them safe. "Yeah." When he got back, first aid kit in hand, he handed the kit to Derrick, then went to Jessica, who had tucked her gun back into her waistband. Drawing her into his arms, he relished the feel of holding her. What if the woman had shot her or Kayla instead of Jessica shooting her?

He didn't want to think about it. Instead, he focused on Derrick, watching as he cleaned the woman's wound and wrapped it in gauze.

"That should do it," Derrick said as he stood.

"What?" the woman said, alarm in her voice. "You're leaving me? Alone?"

Derrick didn't hesitate. "Yeah." He looked at Matt, Jessica, and Kayla. "Let's go."

The four of them left the bathroom to the sounds of the women screaming obscenities.

"I feel bad about leaving her," Jessica murmured to Matt. "I mean, I'm the one who shot her."

Matt turned to her with a frown. "Did you have a good reason to shoot her?"

"Yeah. She had a gun and wanted to kill Kayla."

"Then don't feel bad. Besides, it's not like we can bring her with us. We could never trust her to not hurt Kayla or anyone else in our group."

That seemed to settle Jessica, although he understood

how hard it was to not help someone when in the past they would have helped without hesitation.

They headed straight to the others, who were gathered around Jeff. He was sitting up, leaning against the brick support, a bandage covering his shoulder.

"Are you okay?" Jessica asked him, concern in her voice.

Expression surly, he nodded. "I'll be fine."

Matt lifted his gaze to Emily. She wouldn't pretend everything was okay if it wasn't.

Emily turned to Jessica. "It was a through and through. But still, we have to watch for infection."

"I assume you can walk," Derrick said with a smirk.

Jeff chuckled. "It's my shoulder, not my legs."

"Good. We don't know if any other hostiles are in the area, so we need to get moving."

With help from Chris and Emily, Jeff stood. His face was pale. Matt hoped he wasn't hurt worse than he was letting on.

"Let's blow this pop stand," Jeff said with a laugh.

Matt was ready to leave this rest stop that had been anything but restful. Soon, they were back on I-80 heading west, but this time Derrick was in the lead and Emily drove her and Jeff's truck.

Driving in silence, Matt left Jessica and the kids to their thoughts.

"I can't believe I shot that woman," Jessica said after twenty minutes.

Kayla leaned forward from the back seat, leaning halfway into the front. "You saved me, Mom. That woman said 'A life for a life.' That means she was going to *kill* me." She shook her head. "You had no choice."

Jessica sighed.

"Besides," Kayla added, "she'll be fine. Right, Dad?"

Matt had no idea. If she was really alone, who knew? Still, no reason to make his wife feel guilty for something she'd had to do. "Yeah."

"See, Mom?"

"Now Mom's the badass," Dylan said with respect.

Matt reached over and squeezed Jessica's hand. "That's right."

She smiled at him. "Thanks."

The walkie squawked from the dashboard. Derrick said, "Nevada border five miles ahead. No idea what we might run into so be on alert. Over."

CHAPTER 11

Derrick

DERRICK SET the walkie on the seat beside him. He was still angry with himself for stopping at that rest area, a location with so many potential hiding places. It had been an idiotic decision. One that had gotten Jeff shot. Yes, he should recover, but what if he'd been killed? Or what if someone else in their group had been killed or seriously injured? It could have been catastrophic.

He wouldn't make the same mistake again.

No, you'll make all new ones.

Shaking his head in irritation, he turned his focus to the road ahead. They were rapidly approaching Wendover, the small town that straddled the Utah and Nevada border. They passed the Bonneville Speedway. Only a few more miles. Not that it mattered much. They still had hundreds of miles to go before they reached the farm in California's San Joaquin Valley.

Derrick squinted at the road ahead, then he snatched the

walkie and pressed Talk while sliding his foot to the brake pedal and applying gentle pressure. "Roadblock ahead. Hang back while I approach."

"Copy."

Glancing in his rearview mirror to verify that the rest of the group was stopping, he slowly crept forward. His gaze went to the overpass a quarter of a mile ahead. He wasn't certain, but he thought he'd seen the glint of the sun on metal. The roadblock was on their side of the overpass. Most likely there were also men on the overpass assigned to over-watch. Only the westbound lanes—the way they were traveling—were blocked. Evidently these people didn't want anyone to enter their town, but they were fine with people leaving.

As he got closer to the roadblock—two garbage trucks nose to nose—he saw movement near the rear of one of the trucks. He and his group had to get past this roadblock. They were committed to taking I-80. If they couldn't get through, their only alternative was to take Highway 50, and to access that, they'd have to backtrack all the way to Salt Lake City. That was not an option.

How many men were guarding this roadblock? More than the one man he'd seen, he was certain of that. That, plus the men on the overpass, meant he had no choice but to reason with whomever was in charge.

He pulled to a stop a hundred yards from the roadblock and threw his truck in Park. He took his Glock and holster out of the waistband of his jeans and dropped them to the floor, pushing them under his seat with his foot, then put on his face mask. Next, he rolled his window down and stuck both hands out his window to show he wasn't a threat. He expected that someone—probably several people—had eyes on him at that very moment. Eyes that included at least one pair of binoculars. They would know he was alone.

"Step out of your vehicle," a male voice said over a megaphone. "Keep your hands visible."

Derrick couldn't see where the voice had come from. Using his right hand, he reached through his open window for the outside handle of his door and lifted. The door opened. Using his foot, he pushed the door open farther and swung his feet to the asphalt. With his hands in the air, he stepped out. He loathed the way he was fully exposed. Especially when he had no idea of the intent of these men.

"Step away from the truck," the voice said.

He did so.

"Lift your shirt and turn in a slow circle."

Glad he'd removed his gun—he didn't want to give them a reason to distrust him and he didn't want them to take his weapon—he lifted his shirt and spun in a slow circle.

"Approach slowly."

Derrick let his shirt fall into place, then cautiously walked toward the roadblock. No one was visible. They were smart not to expose themselves.

Was it possible that the man behind the megaphone was all alone? Was this all for show?

When Derrick was ten feet from the roadblock, a nearby voice said, "Stop there."

Holding his hands straight out to his sides, Derrick stopped.

A man in full tactical gear trotted up to him and patted him down, then, while keeping his eyes on Derrick, called out, "He's clean."

A voice answered, "Bring him back."

Okay. So, he wasn't alone. Too bad. That would have made this a lot easier.

The man who'd searched him rested his right hand on the butt of the gun at his hip. He gestured with his head toward the garbage truck. "This way."

Derrick nodded once, then strode past the man. He was curious now to meet the man in charge. The fact that they hadn't shot him led him to believe that they weren't hostile. If not, what was their story?

He walked around the back of the garbage truck, the faint stench of rotten garbage wafting into his nostrils. Rounding the truck, he came face to face with a man who looked to be in his forties, average height, but fit. Behind him stood four other men. All were armed. With a quick glance at the overpass above them, he saw one rifle pointing at him and one pointing toward the westbound lanes where the rest of his group had stopped. A total of eight men. Two in a superior position and the rest well protected behind the garbage trucks.

Great.

"What's your name?" the man in charge asked.

Derrick shifted his gaze to the man. "Derrick. Yours?"

The man pursed his lips like he was deciding if Derrick was worth answering. "Tyson."

Not wanting to give anything away, Derrick stayed silent, staring at the man.

Tyson blinked. "Where are you headed?"

"Just passing through."

Tyson narrowed his eyes. "How many in your group?"

No way was Derrick going to reveal that information. "Are you gonna let us through or what?"

Scowling, Tyson looked at a man to his right. That man gave a slight nod.

Was he the actual person in charge?

Shifting his gaze back to Derrick, Tyson said, "Come back in an hour and we'll talk."

Scrubbing a hand over his face, Derrick withheld a sigh. "What's the problem, Tyson?"

A smile bloomed on Tyson's lips. "No problem. Just need to discuss some things."

Obviously, these people wanted to prove they were in control. Truth was, they were. Reminding himself to relax his jaw, Derrick said, "One hour." Then he turned to walk away.

"Hey," Tyson said from behind him.

Derrick turned to him with a frown.

"You're not going to do anything stupid, are you?"

Derrick couldn't help himself. Grinning, he said, "Never know." He strode away, acutely aware of the guns pointed at his back.

CHAPTER 12

Chris

THE MORE PROBLEMS they ran in to, the more Chris questioned his decision to come on this journey, although he silently acknowledged that if he and his family had stayed they wouldn't necessarily be any better off. Not after he'd turned on the men of the neighborhood co-op. Men who'd gone way over the line, setting fire to Matt's, Derrick's, and Jeff's houses all because they'd refused to go along with their strong-arm tactics to take over the neighborhood. Yeah, he really hadn't had any choice. Coming with this group had been the only play he could make to keep his family safe. And his family was his top priority.

He looked at Amy, who was trying to comfort Aaron, their nearly two-year-old son. Aaron was fussy and unhappy, wanting to get out of his car seat. Both Aaron and six-year-old Jacob were having a rough time. Under the best of circumstances they didn't like being stuck in their car seats for more than a couple of hours. On top of that, he was sure they could feel the tension all around them.

Amy wasn't faring much better. She turned to him with a look of despair. "The boys need a break." She frowned. "So do I." Leaning toward him, she murmured, "One without bullets flying."

Grimacing, he nodded. "I know."

They were waiting for Derrick to negotiate a way through the roadblock, but he'd gone behind the garbage trucks and was no longer visible, which made Chris extremely nervous. For all he knew, Derrick was dead and the rest of them would be next. "Let me see what's going on."

Amy nodded, then gently touched his arm. "Be careful."

He kissed her. "I will." He got out and cautiously looked around. His car was behind Jeff and Emily's, which was behind Matt and Jessica's.

Easing forward, Chris made his way to Jeff and Emily's truck. Emily was behind the wheel and Jeff was stretched out on the backseat, asleep.

"Hey," Chris said to Emily through her open window. "How's Jeff doing?"

She glanced toward the back seat where Jeff was gently snoring. "It's hard to say. He never complains, but the fact that he's asleep says a lot." She smiled at Chris. "He's tough so I'm sure he'll be fine." Her expression sobered. "He has to be."

Chris nodded in agreement. They needed Jeff.

Emily's eyebrows puckered as she turned her eyes toward the front of their caravan. "What's going on up there?"

"Don't know." Chris glanced toward Matt's truck. "Matt probably has a better vantage point."

Emily opened her door and stepped out. "I'll come with you."

The two of them walked toward the driver's side of Matt's truck, keeping close to his RV to keep out of range of anyone pointing a gun their way. Matt must have seen them coming, because he got out and walked in their direction.

"Let's talk over here," Chris said, gesturing to the area behind Matt's RV. It would give them cover while they spoke.

The three of them huddled behind the RV.

"How long's this going to take?" Matt asked.

Chris had no idea, but he didn't like waiting any more than Matt did. "No clue, but I don't like that we can't see what's happening." He didn't want to share his fears with them. No reason to incite panic.

Moments later Jessica came around the side of the RV, her expression hopeful. "Derrick's coming."

That got Chris's attention. "Is he alone?"

"Yes."

Without waiting for any other information, Chris hustled to the front of the truck on the driver's side. Sure enough, there was Derrick, striding toward them with pinched lips and tense shoulders.

Chris waited where he was with Matt, Jessica, and Emily joining him. Derrick looked their way and shifted direction slightly to meet them by the truck.

"What happened?" Matt asked as soon as Derrick was close enough to hear him.

Derrick shook his head, his expression broadcasting annoyance. "Not much."

What did that mean?

Derrick glanced behind them, toward the roadblock, then

faced their group. "They have eight men that I saw, two on overwatch."

"Are they going to let us through?" Emily asked.

Huffing a laugh, Derrick shook his head. "The guy in charge—Tyson—said to come back in an hour and he'd let me know."

Emily pinched the skin at her throat. "What?"

Scowling, Derrick said, "Yeah. Evidently they have to discuss it."

Running her hands through her long hair, Emily sighed. "Why can't they just let us through? Jeff needs proper medical care. We don't have time to sit here while these people have a tea party."

Derrick chuckled and Chris smiled. He wished Jeff was whole and healthy. They could use him about now.

"How's he doing?" Jessica asked, her eyebrows tugging together.

Emily glanced at Chris, then shifted her eyes to Jessica. "He's sleeping right now so it's hard to say."

"Does he have a fever?" Jessica asked.

"Not so far."

Jessica smiled. "That's good."

Derrick looked at them. "We ought to take advantage of the break, but we need to keep watch too."

Amy would be thrilled for the break, especially for the chance to get the kids out of the car for a while. Although he doubted her idea of a break was letting the kids play on the Interstate.

"Let me check on Amy and the kids," Chris said, "and then I'll take watch."

Derrick shook his head. "No. You have a family to care for. I'll take watch."

"I can help," Matt said.

Derrick smiled at him. "Sounds good."

They split up, Chris going to tell Amy the good news.

CHAPTER 13

Jessica

GLAD FOR THE break despite being stopped in the middle of I-80 and having at least eight armed men watching them from afar, Jessica tried to pretend they were on their way to go camping, pulled onto the side of the road to get a snack out of the RV, something they'd done many times before. Of course they'd never stopped right in the middle of the highway.

"Who's hungry?" she asked the kids after opening the rear passenger door of the truck.

They looked at her like she was certifiable, so she explained the situation. Dylan practically leapt from the truck. "I'm going to help Dad keep watch."

She frowned as he raced past her, but she didn't stop him.

"I'm hungry," Kayla said, which reminded Jessica that rather than eating her meager breakfast that morning, Kayla had saved it to give to someone in need. Someone who had ended up shooting at them.

Brooke got out with Cleo and Kayla followed.

"I'll fix something to eat in the RV," Jessica said. She walked back toward the RV, then saw Amy and her two small children getting out of their SUV. She unlocked the door to the RV and pulled down the steps, then headed toward Amy and her family. The younger boy was crying, but the older boy was focused on collecting rocks from the asphalt.

"Hi there," Jessica said to Amy. "You're welcome to join me in the RV if you'd like."

Amy smiled as she touched Jessica's forearm. "That would be wonderful. Thank you." Amy turned to her older boy. "Jake, do you want to see inside that RV?"

Jake stood with two rocks in his hand, an enthusiastic smile spreading across his lips. "Okay."

Glad she could brighten someone's day, even if it was by doing something so small, Jessica led the way to the RV. She climbed in first and pressed the buttons to push out the slide-outs, doubling the interior space of the RV. "Come on in," she called to Amy and her boys.

"Whoa!" Jake said as he climbed inside. "This is so cool!"

Amy followed, setting Aaron on the floor. He immediately toddled away as be began exploring the space.

"Thank you again," Amy said. "I'd much rather they play in here than on the road."

Warmth filled Jessica's chest. "You're welcome." She swept her hand toward the couch. "Make yourself at home." Glancing toward the bathroom, she smiled. "There's a bathroom in there if you need it." Jessica pulled two water bottles out of the pantry, handing one to Amy.

"Thank you." Tears filled Amy's eyes. "I have to admit, this makes me miss the comforts of home."

Before Jessica had a chance to answer, Cleo came bounding inside with Brooke and Kayla right behind her.

Cleo went right to Jake, who giggled as Cleo tried to lick him.

"Come on, girl," Brooke said, snapping her fingers. Cleo came to Brooke's side and sat down, her tail wagging.

Jessica took out three bottles of water and held them out to Kayla. "Take these to Dad, Dylan, and Derrick, would you?"

"Sure, Mom," Kayla said with a happy smile.

Jessica watched her go, worried that she was suppressing her emotions after the terrible events at the rest stop. She'd tried talking to her as they'd driven after leaving the rest stop, but Kayla had insisted she was fine.

Turning her attention to Amy's older son, Jessica asked, "Would you like something to eat, Jake?"

He nodded as he slid onto one of the four chairs surrounding the table. Wishing she had more variety to offer, Jessica asked him if he'd like peanut butter on crackers. He nodded with enthusiasm. She fixed his food, filling a plastic cup with water from a water bottle and setting it in front of him. By then Kayla had returned.

"Everything okay out there?" Jessica asked.

Kayla nodded. "Yeah." She turned to Amy. "Your husband said he was going to stay outside and help keep watch."

Amy softly chuckled. "Figures. Chris can't help himself. He has to be involved."

Jessica thought about Chris coming into their home as part of the neighborhood cooperative, there to forcibly collect food because Dr. Larsen had stitched up Kayla's cut finger. He'd clearly been reluctant to take their food, even making a point of saying he wasn't going to ask if they had food in other places besides the pantry and basement—which they had. She was glad he and his family were on this trek with them. And she was glad she was able to give Amy and her children some relief.

"What can I get you?" she asked Amy, then she listed off the options—crackers, peanut butter, a little bit of cheddar cheese. They also had their freeze-dried pouches, but those were reserved for breakfast and dinner.

"Whatever you have is fine," Amy said.

Jessica fixed a small meal of crackers and cheese as well as more crackers with peanut butter, and they all ate.

Once they'd cleaned up, Kayla and Brooke took Cleo outside, leaving Jessica and Amy alone in the RV with Jake and Aaron. Jessica found paper and crayons for the boys to color with while Jessica sat on a recliner and Amy sat on the couch.

"Do you think we'll make it to California?" Amy asked, her forehead creased with worry.

The same question had crossed Jessica's mind more than once. They'd left home only that morning, and in the time it usually took to get halfway across Nevada, they hadn't even crossed the Nevada state line. Not to mention all the times they'd been shot at. She considered them lucky that only one person in their group had been injured. So far.

Even so, she wanted to reassure Amy, who was about ten years younger than she was. "Eventually, yes."

"Have you been there before?"

"Only to Southern California. You know, to Disneyland and such."

Amy nodded. "Same here." She bit her lip. "Do you think

Emily's aunt and uncle will really be okay with all of us staying at their farm?"

Jessica couldn't tell if Amy was more nervous about the trip or the destination. She wasn't sure herself which worried her more. "Let's not get ahead of ourselves. Let's just focus on what's in front of us." After all, they would have plenty of other things to worry about before they ever got there.

Amy nodded.

Matt stuck his head in the door. "It's been an hour. Derrick's heading back to talk to Tyson."

Jessica's heart lurched. What if this Tyson told them they couldn't pass? Or worse, what if they killed Derrick? What would happen then?

CHAPTER 14

Derrick

WITH EACH STEP HE TOOK, Derrick's dread grew. Tyson held their lives in his hands. Particularly Jeff's life. Derrick had checked in with Emily, and though she'd put on a brave face, when he'd checked on Jeff himself, he could see he wasn't doing great. Jeff had woken when Derrick had spoken to him.

"Hey man," Jeff had said with a wan smile. He was pale and his dressings were tinged with blood.

"How're you doing?"

"I'm awesome." He lifted his head. "Where are we? Why're we stopped?"

"Just outside Wendover. Hit a roadblock." He forced a confident smile. "Don't worry. I've got it handled."

Jeff laid his head back. "Okay then. We'll be fine."

Now, as Derrick approached the garbage trucks, his gaze swept upward to the overpass. Four men were on overwatch now. Great, they'd doubled their numbers up there. Had they taken men from behind the roadblock, or brought in rein-forcements? If he was in charge, he would have brought in more men.

"Stop there," a voice said in a commanding tone when Derrick was ten feet from the roadblock.

He paused.

"Shirt up and turn around."

He knew the drill and he did as they asked, dropping his shirt into place when he'd made a full rotation.

The same man who'd searched him before came out and patted him down once again. "This way."

Derrick followed him, coming around the rear of the garbage truck to find Tyson and a dozen armed men waiting.

Heart pounding, Derrick squeezed his lips together to force away a frown.

"Hope you had a nice break," Tyson said with a wide smile.

Derrick didn't respond.

Tyson's smile faded. "We talked it over and we decided we'd let you through."

Relief burst inside him.

"However," Tyson said, squelching Derrick's hope that they could get through this unscathed, "there is one condition."

Of course there was.

"We require a tax of two pounds of food for every person let through." Tyson grinned. "We counted..." He turned to another man.

"Eleven," the man said.

Tyson faced Derrick. "Eleven people in your group. So, your total tax is twenty-two pounds of food."

Reminding himself to relax his jaw, it took all of Derrick's self-discipline not to slam his fist into Tyson's grinning face. Then he held back a smirk. They actually had twelve people in their group, but Jeff hadn't left the car the entire time they'd been waiting. Whoever had been watching them and counting had missed Jeff.

"That's a lot of food," Derrick said, his tone even.

"Yes. Enough to feed my men dinner tonight." Tyson's gaze swept over the men arrayed around them, clearly trying to emphasize the fact that there were many more of them than there were of Derrick's group.

Derrick did the math. There were sixteen men in Tyson's group, all armed. Whereas his group had six healthy adults, including Jessica, Amy, and Emily. In all reality, he didn't think Jessica or Amy would be up to the challenge of a gunfight. He didn't know about Emily.

Cold, hard math slapped him in the face. They were outnumbered four to one. Fighting their way through the roadblock wasn't an option.

"That's more food than we can spare." In a way, that was a lie. They had a lot of food. But they also had a long way to go. Who knew how many other towns would require a "tax" to pass through? And who knew how long it would take them to arrive at their destination? They had to survive until they got there. Perhaps even after reaching Emily's aunt and uncle's farm they would need the food. For all he knew, her aunt and uncle had no extra. They might even be dead. No, he needed to do whatever he could to reduce this ridiculous tax.

"We can spare five pounds." Derrick grimaced like this offer caused a lot of pain, although it would only be about five cans of vegetables or chili. He hated giving them even that much—it was extortion after all—but they had to get through.

Tyson laughed long and hard, his head tilting back and his mouth opening wide. If it was just the two of them—or even if there'd only been two or three other men besides Tyson— Derrick would take this opportunity to beat the man until he begged for mercy. Instead, he gritted his teeth and waited for Tyson's laughter to subside.

Eyes watering with tears, Tyson chuckled a moment longer, then smiled at Derrick. "Tell you what. We'll settle on fifteen pounds of food and two guns plus ammo." He winked. "We know you must have at least a few guns."

They had more than a few. Each person in their group, minus Chris and Amy's little ones, had a gun either tucked in their waistband or on the seat beside them.

Derrick ground his teeth together. "No deal." Then, with his heart pounding in his throat—would his bluff work or would he end up with a bullet in his back?—he spun on his heel and stalked away.

He hadn't gone more than five steps when Tyson's voice rang out. "Hold up, hold up."

Biting back a relieved smile, Derrick stopped and turned, his eyes on Tyson as the man strode up to him with a smile he probably thought was disarming, but only looked smarmy.

"No need to rush off," Tyson said. "I'm sure we can come to some sort of agreement."

Tyson must have been a politician. Before. Except he still acted like one.

Derrick crossed his arms over his chest. "Eight pounds

and no guns. That's my final offer." Giving away even that much irked him.

A man tapped Tyson on the shoulder—the same man who'd patted Derrick down both times. Tyson turned to look at him. Some sort of silent message passed between them. Tyson swiveled to face Derrick. "You know, if we wanted to, we could take everything you have."

Alarmed at the implied threat, Derrick tilted his head and narrowed his eyes. "Is that a threat?"

Tyson waved his arms like it was all a big misunderstanding. "Of course not. Just pointing out the facts."

"Uh-huh."

"Back to our required tax. Two pounds per person times eleven people equals twenty-two pounds." He chuckled. "Or maybe you'd like to leave some of your people behind. I'm sure you must have some dead weight in your group."

An image of each person traveling with him flashed in Derrick's mind. He'd grown to care about each and every one of them. The idea that he'd leave even one of them behind rankled. "Turns out we've changed our minds."

Tyson's eyes lit up like he was going to get his way.

Derrick held back a grin. "We no longer need to pass through your little town."

Tyson's eyes went wide and his mouth fell open.

Shaking his head, Derrick turned to go, but before he took a step, a hand clamped onto his right upper arm. On instinct, Derrick swung his right arm up and around, breaking the man's grip, while at the same time he swung an uppercut with his left. When Derrick's fist connected with the man's jaw, the man fell back with a grunt. It was the man who'd patted him down.

It felt good to land a punch on one of these goons, but before he had a chance to celebrate, he was taken down from behind by at least two men, the side of his face pressed into the rough asphalt.

"That was a mistake," Tyson said from somewhere above him.

CHAPTER 15

Matt

IT HAD BEEN fifteen minutes since Derrick had gone to talk to the people on the other side of the roadblock. Way too long. Matt looked at the others in his group, who were all gathered near his truck. All except Jeff, who was still stretched out on the back seat of his truck.

"I don't like this," Chris murmured.

Matt glanced at Chris, then let his gaze wander over the rest of their group. With Jeff out of commission and Derrick doing who knew what, he and Chris were the only men left. He was all for women fighting just as hard as men, but there was no way he'd send Jessica—or Amy or Emily for that matter—into the midst of the men blocking their way. They knew very little about these people's motives or tactics. How many were there? What were they capable of?

Matt rubbed the back of his neck. "I don't either."

"Attention," a voice shouted over a megaphone.

Matt glanced at Chris, whose eyebrows tugged together.

They all turned toward the source of the voice, toward the roadblock.

"One of you approach. Unarmed."

Heart rate climbing, Matt shifted his gaze to Chris. "What do you think's going on? Where's Derrick?"

Chris shook his head. "No idea, but this can't be good."

Matt agreed. Why would they ask for someone else to come over if Derrick was already there negotiating? Unless something had gone awry.

"Now," the voice demanded.

Matt looked at Chris and Chris looked back.

"I'll go," Chris said.

Amy grabbed his arm, her tone shot-through with worry. "No."

Matt looked at Amy and her two young children. If anything happened to Chris, she would be on her own. Then he looked at Jessica and their children. If anything happened to him, she would be devastated. Still, their children were older, more independent.

It had to be him.

He shook his head at Chris. "No. I'll go."

"Matt," Jessica said, her voice shaky.

Turning to her with a reassuring smile—a false smile—he said, "It'll be fine."

Her lips flattened. "You don't know that."

No. He didn't. But what other option was there?

He kissed her, handed his .45 to Chris, then pulled on a face mask. "I'll be back as soon as I can."

With a grim smile, Chris nodded.

Forcing confidence he was nowhere near feeling, Matt strode toward the roadblock. Guns, seen and unseen, were pointing at him. And he was unarmed and completely vulnerable. Had they already killed Derrick? Was he next? Was he walking into a trap? Would he leave Jessica a widow before they'd even left the state of Utah?

Heart jackhammering so hard that it made him cough, he nearly stumbled on the asphalt. He glanced behind him at his family. Jessica's eyes were wide and one hand was pressed to her mouth. Trying to reassure her, Matt nodded, then he faced forward and breathed in and out, slow and steady. He had to get his slamming heart under control before he went into cardiac arrest.

Ten feet from where the garbage trucks met, a voice shouted for him to stop, lift his shirt, and turn slowly. That did nothing to calm him. Regardless, he did as they asked, then a man darted out and patted him down before demanding that Matt follow him.

Forcing one leg in front of the other, he followed the man past the back of the garbage truck and around the side. That's when he saw Derrick lying helpless on the asphalt, hands bound behind his back and duct tape covering his mouth.

Panic blasted through him. Why had they tied Derrick up? What were they going to do to *him*?

Mentally pointing out that Derrick was still alive, he let his gaze glide over the men standing in a loose semi-circle. All were armed, and all looked angry. Then he noticed that one man was holding his jaw like he was in pain. Had Derrick punched the guy?

In all the horrible events Matt had been in with Derrick, he'd never seen Derrick hit someone. What had happened?

Matt's eyes went back to Derrick. His face mask was

nowhere to be seen. And these guys weren't wearing any protection on their faces. Were they all healthy?

Swallowing over his panic, he looked at the assembled men. "Which one of you is Tyson?"

A man stepped forward, his expression less than friendly. "I'm Tyson. Who are you?"

"Matt." Matt let his eyes slide to Derrick to get some indication of what was going on, but with his mouth covered with duct tape, Derrick only stared back. Matt shifted his gaze to Tyson. "What happened?"

The corners of Tyson's lips tugged upward. "Negotiations broke down so we decided it might be helpful to have a new negotiator."

Oh crap! If Tyson didn't like Matt's answers, he'd end up on the ground next to Derrick. He shoved down his fear. "I see."

"Like I told your friend Derrick," Tyson said as he glanced toward Derrick, whose eyes narrowed in obvious anger, "we require a tax from all those who wish to pass through."

It felt like a boulder had been deposited in Matt's stomach. "What kind of tax?"

Tyson glanced at Derrick again before facing Matt. "Three pounds of food for each person passing through." He grinned. "Once you deliver the tax, we'll let your friend go."

Derrick made a noise like he was trying to yell something. Matt desperately wished he knew what it was.

"That's thirty-three pounds," Tyson said, his voice calm like he was in complete control, which, since he had a dozen armed men backing him up, he was.

Though Matt knew very well that they had twelve people in their group, Matt wasn't going to point out Tyson's mathematical error. "We don't have that much," he said instead.

That wasn't true, but he wasn't about to let on to how much they actually had.

Sighing heavily, like he'd been through all of this before, Tyson shook his head. "Come now, Matt. You and I both know you're lying."

What exactly had Derrick told him? There was no way Derrick would have told these people any more than the bare minimum. No. Tyson was bluffing.

"I'm sorry," Matt said, putting as much sorrow into his voice as he could muster, "I wish we had that much, but we simply don't."

Tyson's nostrils flared. "Do we need yet another negotiator?"

Tamping down the panic that pushed at the edges of his mind, Matt took a step back. "I'm sure we can come to some sort of agreement."

"I hope so. This is getting tiresome."

Matt wasn't exactly having a good time either. This was reminiscent of the neighborhood cooperative coming to his house and taking twenty percent of all he had. That hadn't ended well.

As much as it infuriated Matt to be strong-armed by anyone, he was eager to get this resolved. "I can offer you twelve pounds of food."

Without even thinking it over, Tyson shook his head. "That's not enough, Matt. Not nearly enough."

Gritting his teeth, Matt said, "What's the least amount you'll accept?"

Tapping his chin with his finger, Tyson thought it over. "I suppose an even two dozen pounds would do it."

Derrick thrashed on the ground as he shouted something

against the duct tape.

With the sinking feeling that he was being taken, Matt didn't know what else to do besides give in to Tyson's demands. The man held all the cards, and, Matt told himself, at least he wasn't asking for weapons or the RV.

Sighing audibly, Matt nodded. "Okay. I'll get the food, then you let Derrick go and let us pass without harm."

A wide smile curved Tyson's lips. "You have a deal."

CHAPTER 16

Derrick

FURIOUS THAT TYSON had managed to get more food out of Matt than he'd originally asked for from Derrick, Derrick felt his blood start to boil. Making matters worse, his hands were zip-tied behind his back. He was no action hero. There was nothing he could do but wait for Matt to come back with the coveted food. Besides, they were so close to getting past Wendover, he didn't want to screw it up by doing something stupid. Instead, he would have to force himself to chill.

He lay on the hard asphalt for a long time—thirty minutes, he guessed—before Matt came back with a box filled with cans of food. During that time, Tyson's men had never talked about anything useful, much to Derrick's disappointment. He'd been hoping they would say something that he could use against them, but no luck.

With a wide smile, Tyson took the box from Matt. He didn't even say thank you.

Watching the exchange in forced silence, Derrick looked

at Matt's pinched lips and tight expression and knew he was just as angry as Derrick was. Then again, people taking his food had led Matt to take a stand back home. This was different though. These people had greater numbers, superior position, and better cover. And no right.

It rankled. Badly. But there was nothing they could do but swallow their pride and get on with their lives.

"I brought the food," Matt said, "now, let Derrick go."

Tyson laughed. "Not yet, friend."

Matt scowled. "Why not?"

Tyson threw his thumb toward Derrick. "Your buddy can't be trusted not to attack my men. So, I'll tell you how this is going to go." Tyson smiled. "We will escort you and your group to the other end of town. One of my men will drive Derrick's truck while Derrick rides with us." He glanced at Derrick. "Keys in the ignition?"

Derrick listened with growing rage, his eyes narrowing. With duct tape covering his mouth, he couldn't answer Tyson.

Matt looked Derrick's way, his face grim. He nodded. "Fine." Tyson smiled. Matt turned and walked away, leaving Derrick alone.

Someone roughly pulled Derrick to his feet. As much as he wanted to throw a roundhouse kick, with a dozen armed men surrounding him, he smothered his need for revenge and let them lead him to a truck parked off to the side.

While one man gripped Derrick's upper arm, another man with a scraggly beard and mean eyes opened the rear passenger door of the truck before turning to Derrick. "Get in." He held his gun steady on Derrick, his expression making Derrick believe he wanted a reason to shoot.

Derrick slid inside. Scraggly Beard ripped the duct tape

from Derrick's mouth, then closed the door behind him. Derrick was left alone.

Swearing under his breath at the sting left by the tape being torn from his face, Derrick glared at Scraggly Beard, who stood outside the door of the truck, his eyes shifting between Derrick and the other activities going on. Derrick watched as the two garbage trucks were backed out of the way, creating an opening wide enough for a single line of vehicles to pass through. He couldn't see Matt and the rest of their group.

Ten minutes later, Tyson appeared at Derrick's door, pulling it open with a grin. "Look what I found." He held up a Glock 21. The same one Derrick had tucked under his seat a few hours earlier. The same one he always carried in his concealed carry holster. It was his favorite gun.

"That's mine," Derrick said, his voice deadly calm.

Tyson's smile grew. "Not anymore. It's payment for the injury you caused my man."

Jaw aching from clenching it so hard, Derrick glared at Tyson. "Your man deserved it."

The smile melted from Tyson's face. "We don't condone violence here."

Tilting his head, Derrick paused, then burst out laughing. "Right."

Looking offended, Tyson shook his head then turned to leave.

"Hey."

He stopped and looked at Derrick.

"I'll expect to get my gun back when we reach the other side of town."

91

Tyson narrowed his eyes, then he pursed his lips before closing the door and stalking away.

More livid than ever, when three men got in the truck, including Scraggly Beard, who climbed in back and pointed his gun at Derrick's head, Derrick had to remind himself to breathe slow and deep.

"Everything okay?" Scraggly Beard asked him, his tone snide.

Sliding his eyes to his back seat neighbor before looking toward the front again, Derrick didn't reply.

Just then, Derrick's truck came into view driven by one of Tyson's men. Tyson sat in the passenger seat.

"Nice ride," Scraggly Beard said. "I wouldn't mind owning it."

Derrick didn't take the bait, his eyes on Matt and his RV, followed by Emily, then Chris. Jeff wasn't visible.

The man driving the truck Derrick was riding in pulled into line behind Chris's SUV. They slowly made their way forward, passing a Welcome to Nevada sign. Just over the border, a casino sat on the left. They drove on, not stopping until they were several miles west of Wendover.

Their caravan came to a halt. The truck Derrick was in passed the parade of cars, pulling to a stop beside Derrick's truck. Tyson and the man who'd driven Derrick's truck stood outside.

With his hands bound, Derrick had to wait for Scraggly Beard to get out and come around to open his door. The door swung open and Scraggly Beard pointed his gun at Derrick. "Get out."

More than happy to comply, Derrick swung his legs out of the door and hopped out. Tyson was walking his way,

Derrick's gun tucked into the front waistband of his jeans. All four of Tyson's men who had come along stood in a half-circle, guns ready, but aimed at the ground. Derrick was completely outgunned, but this was the only chance he was going to get against these bullies. He wanted to make them pay for their extortion, wanted to make sure they didn't continue stealing from innocent travelers.

Derrick stared Tyson down. "You gonna undo my hands?"

A smile pulled up the corners of Tyson's lips. "You've been a good boy, so yeah." Tyson nodded at one of his men, who cut the zip ties from Derrick's wrists.

Forcing a friendly smile, Derrick held out his hand to Tyson, whose smile widened as his hand came up automatically.

Holding back a grin, Derrick slid his hand into Tyson's, then abruptly yanked him forward, spinning him around so that his back was to Derrick. At the same time, he snatched his gun from Tyson's waistband. Using Tyson as a shield, Derrick held the gun to Tyson's head.

The four men who'd come with Tyson raised their guns and pointed them at Derrick, but they couldn't shoot him without hitting Tyson.

Tyson trembled, ever so slightly.

"Tell your men to drop their weapons," Derrick growled in his ear.

"D...drop your weapons." Tyson stammered the command without a moment's hesitation, all his bravery gone now that he wasn't the tough guy holding the gun.

Scraggly Beard narrowed his eyes, his gun still trained on Derrick.

Derrick was so done with these people. "Do it now!"

Tyson nodded. "Do it."

Looking furious, the men dropped their guns to the pavement.

Derrick softly exhaled. "Kick them over here."

The men complied.

Matt and Chris joined Derrick, much to Derrick's relief. Chris pointed his gun at Tyson's men while Matt collected the guns from the pavement.

With a grim smile at his friends, and with Tyson still in his grip, Derrick looked at Tyson's men. "All of you, turn around and put your hands on your heads." They did so before Matt and Chris quickly patted them down, coming up with two knives and another gun.

Matt and Chris stepped back and trained their guns on the men. Derrick released Tyson before shoving him. "Join your men."

Staggering a bit, Tyson made his way to his men, who stood together several yards away.

Derrick stared at them. "Take off your shoes and socks."

With fury in their eyes, they did as instructed.

"Turn around and put your hands behind your backs."

"You're going to regret this," Scraggly Beard breathed out.

"Yeah, yeah. Just do it." Never dropping his aim, Derrick turned to Chris. "Will you search their truck? Look for zip ties."

Chris grinned. "Glad to."

Five minutes later, Chris returned with a handful of zip ties along with another gun. "Found this."

Not surprised, Derrick smirked as he shook his head. He turned to Matt, who was aiming his gun at the five men. "Hold your aim while Chris and I bind their hands."

Matt nodded. "Will do."

Once all of the men had their hands tied behind their backs, Derrick opened the gate on the bed of their truck. "Climb in."

They struggled, but eventually all five were sitting in the bed of the truck.

Derrick closed the gate.

"What are you going to do?" Tyson asked, fear shining from his eyes.

Derrick glanced at the cloudless sky before meeting his gaze. "It's a lovely day for a drive."

Tyson's eyes widened. "Are you going to kill us?"

Derrick wasn't the kind of person to kill someone in cold blood, but they didn't have to know that, so he just smiled, then turned to Matt. "Want to go for a drive?"

Matt looked uncertain, but he nodded.

CHAPTER 17

Matt

KEEPING an eye on the men in the bed of the truck, Matt held on as Derrick drove across the open desert. The ground was bumpy, and as uncomfortable as it was in the cab of the truck, seeing Tyson and his men bouncing in the hard bed of the truck brought Matt a feeling of grim satisfaction. These guys had stolen their food under the guise of a tax. How many other travelers had they victimized?

Matt glanced at Derrick, who was concentrating on where they were driving. "How far are we going?"

Derrick grinned. "Far enough that it'll take them a long, long time to get back to their buddies."

"So, you're not going to shoot them?" Because if Derrick was capable of that, Matt wasn't sure he wanted to be in his group.

Derrick laughed and shook his head. "I know you don't know me all that well, Matt, but I hope you know I wouldn't shoot a man unless I had to."

CHRISTINE KERSEY

Matt felt a mix of embarrassment and shame that the thought had definitely crossed his mind. "Right."

They'd driven several miles before Derrick slowed to a stop. He left the truck running before getting out of the cab. Matt got out as well.

Derrick pulled down the gate on the bed. "Okay. Everyone out."

"Look," Tyson said, his voice nearly a whine, "you don't have to do this. We'll give you your food back."

Derrick lifted his gun and pointed it at Tyson. "Don't make me ask you again."

Tyson scooted toward the gate. "Okay, okay." He jumped to the hard-packed dirt and his men followed.

Derrick used his gun to point to an area several yards away. "Move over there."

The men obeyed and Derrick closed the gate of the truck. He looked at Matt with a grin and motioned with his head to the cab of the truck. "Let's go."

They began walking to their respective doors.

"Wait!"

It was Tyson. At the look of desperation on his face, Matt held back a chuckle.

"You're not going to leave us here, are you?" Tyson asked.

Derrick tilted his head. "If you prefer, I can shoot you."

"No, no. That's fine. We can walk."

"Yep." Derrick turned and lifted the handle to the driver's door. Matt got in on the passenger side.

As Tyson and his men faded in the sideview mirror, Matt softly exhaled. That could have gone so very wrong, but it felt good to have bested those jerks.

Eventually they reached the interstate where the rest of their group had waited.

"What happened?" Jessica asked Matt the moment he got out of the truck, her eyes wide.

He couldn't hold back a laugh as he told her what they'd done.

Looking relieved, she said, "They got better than they deserved."

He agreed.

"Jessica," Derrick said, "would you drive my truck for a few miles? I don't want to leave their truck where they can use it."

She smiled. "Sure."

Matt watched Derrick gather the shoes and socks the men had left on the side of the road, tossing them into the bed of the truck, then off they went with Derrick in the lead.

After ten miles, Derrick pulled over, so the rest of them did as well.

Soon enough, Jessica was back in the passenger seat of Matt's truck. He smiled at her.

"That was clever of Derrick," Dylan said. "Now those guys won't be able to catch up with us."

Matt nodded. He was glad Derrick hadn't just left them on the side of the road where they could have easily tracked them down.

Cleo rested her head on the console dividing the two front seats. Matt reached over and scratched the top of her head. Cleo lifted her head and panted as she looked at him. He smiled at her. "You're a good girl." Her tail thumped against the rear seat.

"Ow! Cleo, calm down."

Matt smiled at Kayla, who was sitting between Dylan and Brooke and was getting the brunt of Cleo's enthusiasm. Brooke laughed, but pushed a hand against Cleo's rump, forcing her to sit.

They drove on without incident, occasionally passing cars traveling west as well.

They'd gone about a hundred and fifty miles when the walkie squawked. "I'm running low on gas. Over." It was Chris.

"I, uh..." Emily began, "I think Jeff's running a fever."

"Oh no," Jessica said.

Moments later, Derrick pulled to the shoulder of I-80, half of his truck still in the right-hand lane. Matt followed suit. Right after he turned off his truck, everyone got out. The kids took Cleo for a walk while he and Jessica went to Jeff and Emily's truck, which was right behind them.

"How's he doing?" Jessica asked Emily.

Worry bracketed Emily's eyes. "Not good. He's thrashing around back there and he has a fever."

"We have Tylenol," Jessica said with a grimace. "Maybe that will help."

Emily's forehead was furrowed. "I'll try anything."

If Jeff didn't get better, they'd be in a world of hurt. He'd proven his value many times already. They needed him whole and healthy. Matt cleared his throat. "I'll grab the Tylenol."

Jessica smiled at him. "Thanks."

He got the Tylenol and a bottle of water out of the RV, then gave them to Emily. "Do you need more gas?"

Emily nodded.

Glad he could do something useful, he smiled. "I'll get some for you."

She smiled in appreciation. "Thank you."

He went to Derrick's truck where Derrick had several small containers of gas. Derrick was pouring gas into his tank. Chris was doing the same in his SUV. Glad he had the auxiliary tank on his truck, which would take him hundreds of miles further, Matt stopped beside Derrick. "Do you have enough for Jeff and Emily's truck?"

Grimacing, Derrick nodded. "We have enough to get us to the next town, but we should stop there and fill up if we can."

Matt glanced toward Jeff and Emily's truck. "We need to find some medical help for Jeff."

Derrick looked at Matt sharply. "That bad, huh?"

Matt just shook his head, then he lifted a two-gallon container of gas from the back of Derrick's truck before walking back to Jeff's truck and pouring it into the tank. As he poured, he saw Emily coaxing Jeff to drink some water. Jeff struggled, but managed to swallow some.

Once all the gas had been emptied into tanks, they hit the road. After a while Derrick's voice came over the walkie. "We're coming up on a small town. We'll stop there for gas and medical help. Over."

Matt hoped they could find both.

CHAPTER 18

Jessica

As they exited I-80 and headed toward the town, Jessica's gaze shot in all directions. Wary about someone attacking them, she wished they didn't have to stop at all. But they had to. Jeff needed help—help they couldn't provide. And the others needed gas.

Sagebrush lined both sides of the road, stretching as far as the eye could see. They drove for nearly two miles before they reached the outskirts of town, and to Jessica's pleased surprise, there was a gas station right there.

Following Derrick, they pulled into the station.

"Looks like they have diesel," Matt said as he squinted at the pumps. "We can top off."

"I need to pee," Kayla said.

Jessica turned and smiled at her children. "We can all use a pit stop."

There were only two pumps with two sides to each, so all four of the vehicles were able to stop next to a pump.

Matt shut off the engine and they all got out, including Cleo, who pranced around, happy to be out of the truck.

The mini-mart looked abandoned.

Matt stared at the pump in front of him. "Looks like it's off."

Jessica sighed. "Now what?"

Chris was opposite them. "If there's no generator to run the pump, we're out of luck."

"Can I at least use the bathroom?" Kayla asked. Her eyebrows rose. "Since you don't want us using the one in the RV."

"We need to save the water in the RV for drinking," Jessica said, although she understood Kayla's complaint. "If we can find water to wash down the RV toilet, we can use it."

That seemed to brighten Kayla's mood.

Jessica held back a laugh. The things that made her daughter happy now.

Jessica waited while the men hunted down a generator, but after five minutes they came back with bad news.

"No luck," Matt said with a frown. "We'll have to go farther into town and find another gas station."

"And hope their gas pumps work," Dylan added.

Matt ruffled Dylan's hair. "Yep."

"Hold on a second," Amy said to Chris as she held her younger boy in her arms. "You were able to get inside the mini-mart, right?"

Chris nodded. "Yeah."

Amy's eyebrows rose. She glanced at Jessica. "Well, some of us would like to use the ladies' room."

"Oh," Chris said with chagrined smile. "Right."

Derrick and Matt kept watch while Chris escorted the

rest of the group inside where they not only used the restrooms but gathered several gallons of bottled water.

"We can use it for drinking," Jessica said to Kayla and Brooke as they walked back to the truck, "or in a pinch, we can use it for washing."

A few minutes later they were back on the road, heading west through town.

Occasionally they saw someone outside watching them drive by, but the place was eerily quiet.

"I wonder how many people died here," Brooke murmured.

Jessica didn't want to think about the dead and dying. They were alive and that was all she wanted to focus on.

They passed several mom and pop restaurants and a couple of small motels. A railroad track ran alongside the road to their right. Eventually they reached the other side of town where they found another gas station, this one much larger than the first. It had multiple pumps, including pumps just for semi-trucks.

One man was standing at a pump, filling his car.

"This looks promising," Matt murmured.

Jessica had high hopes as well, although she worried what the gas station would charge. She and Matt had a decent amount of cash with them, but she expected the prices to be sky-high.

All four of them pulled into the lanes, stopping beside pumps, then got out.

A man with a bushy mustache and friendly smile came rushing out to greet them. "Howdy do." His jeans sagged on his hips, but he didn't seem to notice.

"Hi," Matt said with a smile, the mask on his face.

Jessica watched the exchange, relieved to interact with a stranger who wasn't interested in shooting at them for a change.

"We need some fuel," Matt said, sweeping his hand toward the rest of their group.

Derrick, Emily, and Chris joined them, all masked.

"How much for a gallon of unleaded?" Derrick asked, his tone wary.

The man looked at Derrick. "Eight dollars a gallon."

Though that was much higher than it had been before the pandemic, it wasn't nearly as high as Jessica had feared it would be.

"We can do five dollars a gallon," Derrick said. "For all of us."

The man chewed on his lower lip a moment. "I'll do six fifty."

Derrick nodded. "Deal."

"I need diesel," Matt said. "Six fifty for that as well?"

The man paused a second. "Yeah. I can do that for you." He looked at each of them. "Cash only. And I need a deposit of a hundred dollars per vehicle. That'll get you..." He looked up as he did the math. "Fifteen gallons to start."

At least he hadn't asked for them to hand over their food.

Matt, Derrick, and Chris pulled out their wallets. Emily took a step forward. "Do you know of a doctor around here?"

The man stumbled backwards. "Are ya sick with that flu?"

She rapidly shook her head. "No no no. It's my husband. He's injured."

Jessica noticed Emily hadn't mentioned Jeff had been shot. No reason to alarm the man.

He seemed to relax. "Oh. I see. No. Sorry. I can't help you."

Emily's shoulders sagged.

The man filling his car at the adjacent pump stepped forward. Jessica noticed Derrick reaching for his gun.

"I might be able to help," he said.

CHAPTER 19

Derrick

WHO WAS this guy and what were his motives? After all they'd been through, Derrick's trust in strangers was completely gone.

"Thank you," Emily said, her smile bright with relief. She turned to Derrick with hope-filled eyes.

He stared back. He didn't like it, not one bit. But Jeff needed help. Where else were they supposed to turn? Still, things had not gone well that day, not by a mile. If Emily went, they all needed to go.

He clenched his jaw, his gaze going to Jeff, who was asleep in the back seat of the truck. He looked at the man who'd offered help, taking the measure of him. He had a streak of dirt on his face and his cheeks were hollowed out like he hadn't had enough to eat. Was he hungry enough to lure them into danger?

Jeff moaned and all eyes went to him. His head turned from side to side like he was in distress.

"Please, Derrick," Emily whispered.

He watched Jeff. They needed him. More than that, he was a friend. Derrick faced the man. "How can you help?"

"The doc. He's helping people at his house."

That sounded good. If it was true. Derrick considered the other option—keep going and risk Jeff not making it. That wasn't a choice he was willing to make. Besides, it was ultimately up to Emily. He appreciated her looking to him for agreement.

Finally, and with great reluctance, he turned to Emily. "We'll all go."

She whooshed an exhale and spun to face the man who had offered. "If you can wait until we fill up?"

The man smiled, revealing straight white teeth.

Quietly sighing, Derrick turned away and went to his truck to fill it up. By the time everyone had filled their tanks and Matt had topped off his auxiliary tank, Derrick was slightly on edge. Even so, he led the way, following the man who said he could help Jeff.

As they pulled out of the gas station and turned right, back the way they'd just come, he picked up the walkie and pressed Talk. "Be on guard. We don't know if this guy is legit. Over."

Everyone agreed and on they went. The town was tiny, and after only a few minutes and several turns down residential streets, the man pulled into the driveway of a modest house. Eyes scanning, Derrick felt a modicum of relief when it looked like no one was hiding around corners ready to ambush them. The street ahead looked clear—no roadblocks or dead ends. He pulled to a stop at the curb. The others stopped behind him in a long line.

The man got out of his car and looked at Derrick, waving an arm to follow.

He picked up the walkie. "I'll check it out and let you know if it's safe. Over."

Hooking the small walkie talkie onto his back pocket and making sure his Glock was locked and loaded, he got out of his truck and cautiously strode to the front door, where the man was already knocking.

An older man opened the door, a tired smile on his face. To Derrick's surprise, he wasn't masked. "Good afternoon, Tommy."

"Hi, Doc." Tommy jabbed a thumb in Derrick's direction. "Brought some folks over who need some help."

Doc lifted his gaze to Derrick. "That so?"

Everything seemed on the up and up. Derrick felt his body relax. "Yeah. Ran into some nasty people earlier today. My friend..." He gestured toward Jeff's truck, "he got shot."

Doc didn't look surprised. "Been a bit of that going on, I'm afraid. People gettin' desperate and all."

"Can you help him?"

He nodded and waved him in. "Bring him in."

Derrick spoke into the walkie, telling his group to bring Jeff in. He turned to Tommy. "Thanks for helping us."

Tommy smiled. "Glad to."

"Tommy's good folks," Doc said.

To Derrick's surprise, he felt a burst of warmth in his chest, like he'd forgotten there were actually good people in the world, people willing to help without expecting anything in return.

Tommy turned and walked to his car.

"Hold up," Derrick said.

Tommy spun around, a question on his face.

Derrick held up one finger, then jogged to his truck and dug around. A moment later he held up several cans of chili. He trotted over to Tommy and handed him the cans. "Thanks for bringing us here."

Tommy cradled the cans to his chest as a smile lit up his face. "Thanks. This...this means more than you know."

Derrick nodded. It felt good to share by choice instead of by force. "Take care."

Tommy nodded, then climbed into his car and drove off.

By then, Matt and Chris had reached the porch with Jeff between them and Emily right behind them.

"What's going on?" Jeff asked. "Where are we?"

Derrick smiled at him. "Getting you some help, bro."

He shook his head, but he was clearly weak. "I'm fine."

Derrick rolled his eyes. "Right."

"Come on in," Doc said before turning and walking inside the house. Derrick went in first, scanning for trouble before he motioned with his head for the others to follow.

Doc's front room had been turned in to a make-shift doctor's office with an exam table in the center and supplies on nearby shelves and the curtains pulled wide to let the light from the sun stream in.

Derrick helped Chris and Matt get Jeff onto the table, then he turned to the men. "I'll stay with Emily. You guys keep watch outside."

They nodded and left.

"Is he going to be okay?" Emily asked as she hovered near Jeff's head.

Doc leaned close to the bullet wound, angling a flashlight that was hanging overhead so that the beam hit Jeff's left shoulder. "Let's take a look." Jeff was awake but calm as Doc examined his shoulder. "Good news is, I don't see any bullet fragments." Doc straightened and frowned at them. "Bad news is, he needs antibiotics."

Derrick looked at the supplies on the shelves, which was when he realized there weren't any bottles of pills. He lifted his gaze to Doc. "I take it you don't have any."

Doc shook his head. "With all the people who caught that flu, I'm plumb out."

Derrick frowned.

"What's going on with the flu?" Emily asked. "I mean, are people still dying?"

Doc smiled. "Now that's where the flu being a fast killer was a good thing."

Emily's eyebrows shot up. "A good thing? How so?"

Doc shook his head. "People who caught it started dying so quick that they didn't have time to spread it. It's burning itself out."

Emily smiled. "That's great news."

"Yep." He turned his attention back to Jeff. "I can get this cleaned up and sutured, but if he doesn't get those antibiotics, infection is a real concern."

"Where can we get antibiotics?" Derrick asked.

Doc lifted his head and looked at Derrick. "The pharmacy in town should have some." A deep crease formed on Doc's forehead. "Only problem is, a group's taken it over."

That couldn't be good. Derrick highly doubted this group would just hand over what they needed. "What about the neighboring houses? Do you think they'd have any meds?"

Doc shook his head. "I've already had some people search for me. This neighborhood is cleaned out. They all are."

Of course. "How far to the next town? Maybe they have something we could use."

"Doubtful. Anyway, it's a long drive."

Yeah, Derrick had noticed that towns were few and far between along I-80. Looked like they had no option but to deal with the people who had taken over the pharmacy. "What do you know about these guys? Will they negotiate?"

Doc tilted his head. "Hard to say. From the rumors I've heard, they're not real friendly. Taking what they can get for not a lot in return."

Suppressing a sigh, Derrick got the directions to the pharmacy from Doc. "I'll see what I can do." He turned to Emily. "I'll take Chris or Matt and see about getting those antibiotics for Jeff."

She nodded, her expression pinched. "Thank you, Derrick."

Frustrated with all the issues they'd already faced that day —and it was only early afternoon—Derrick turned and left.

CHAPTER 20

Matt

MATT LEANED against his truck and watched Dylan throw a ball for Cleo, who chased after it before retrieving it, a wide doggie smile on her face.

"Good girl, Cleo," Dylan said, ruffling the fur on her head.

It made Matt happy to see a moment of normalcy. At least it seemed normal. Until he looked around at the unfamiliar neighborhood and remembered why they were there. Still, he would take whatever moments of joy he could get.

"Do you think Jeff will be okay?" Kayla asked. She stood near him, as did Jessica and Brooke. It seemed as if no one wanted to stray too far from the relative safety of their group.

He pushed a smile onto his lips. "He's with a doctor, so his chances are good. And the bullet isn't lodged in his shoulder, so that helps too."

Derrick came trotting out of the house wearing that look of all-business he got when there was a problem. Matt straightened and took a deep breath, preparing himself for whatever bad news Derrick was bringing.

"What's up?" Chris asked Derrick, joining Matt and the others. "Is Jeff okay?"

Derrick rubbed the back of his neck. "Yeah, but there's a problem."

Of course there was. Nothing could ever be easy. Not in this new world.

"What's wrong?" Chris asked.

"Jeff needs antibiotics, but the doc doesn't have any. We need to get some from the pharmacy in town." Derrick sighed.

Matt narrowed his eyes. "And?"

Derrick's lips flattened. "Some group took it over."

"Group?" Matt asked. "What group?"

Derrick shook his head. "Not sure."

"Wonderful," Chris muttered.

"Can't we look for antibiotics somewhere else?" Jessica asked, her eyebrows bunched in concern.

Derrick frowned. "Already thought of that. Doc says there's nothing anywhere else. Besides, we need to get Jeff started on them right away." He paused a beat. "If we wait, infection could set in."

It sounded like there wasn't much choice. But what about their recent interaction with Tyson? What if these men were just as bad? What if these people killed one of their group?

"I'm gonna go there." Derrick pursed his lips. "I don't want to endanger any of you, so I'll go by myself."

"No," Matt heard himself say. "You should have backup." He looked at each member of the group. "None of us should ever go into a dangerous situation alone. We should always have backup." He paused a beat. "I'll go with you."

"Matt," Jessica whispered urgently from beside him.

He looked at her, saw the concern on her face, and clasped her hand with his, squeezing gently. "What if it was one of our kids that needed medicine? I know Jeff would do it for them. For any of us."

Her shoulders slumped and she stared at the ground before lifting her eyes to his. "Please be careful."

He kissed her on the lips. "Always."

He shifted his gaze to Derrick, who stared at him and asked, "Are you sure?"

He wasn't sure about anything, except that it wasn't right that Derrick was always the one jumping into danger. They all had to take risks. For each other. That was the only way to survive.

Matt nodded. "Yeah."

A grin tugged up the corners of Derrick's mouth. "Okay then. Let's go. We'll take my truck."

While Matt gave Jessica and the kids a hug, he heard Derrick telling Chris how to get to the pharmacy in case they didn't return within an hour.

"Hey," Matt said with a grin, "just pull it up on your phone."

Everyone laughed. Those days were long gone. It had only been two weeks since their world had shifted, but Matt dearly missed the technology that had been part of his daily life. Ah well, nothing he could do about that now.

As they pulled away from the curb, Matt watched his family recede in his sideview mirror. "How far is it?"

Derrick glanced at him. "Not far. We'll park a couple of blocks away and go the rest of the way on foot. Check things out before we approach these guys."

"Sounds good."

CHAPTER 21

Derrick

T HOUGH D ERRICK HAD BEEN MORE than willing to go to the pharmacy alone, he was actually glad that Matt had volunteered to come along. Even though Matt wasn't experienced in combat, he was learning quickly and becoming a real asset.

Derrick pictured the route to the pharmacy that Doc had shown him on a map. They were close, but they needed a place to hide the truck. A restaurant came into view. Derrick turned into the parking lot. The place looked abandoned. No people. No cars. Perfect.

He parked the truck, then dropped the magazine from his Glock. Fully loaded. He slammed it back into place and looked at Matt, who was checking his weapon as well. "Ready?"

Matt nodded, his expression serious.

They got out of the truck. Derrick tucked his gun into his waist holster, then after grabbing a few cans of food, he and

Matt began walking. When the pharmacy came into view, he glanced at Matt. "Follow my lead."

Two people—a man and a woman—stood in line at a long table just outside the entrance to the pharmacy. The man held a box and the woman held a grocery bag. On the table were cans of food, bottles of water, and other assorted items. Two men stood at either end of the table—one bald and the other smoking a joint. Another man—the clerk?—sat behind the table talking to the customer. A fourth man stood behind the clerk. All four men were armed.

When Derrick and Matt were twenty yards away, Baldy looked their way, hand resting on the butt of his gun and sunglasses obscuring his eyes.

Ignoring him and the other guard, Derrick and Matt walked to the end of the line and stood behind the woman. Wearing sunglasses himself, Derrick kept an eye on every person within view. His gaze went to the glass doors that led to the interior of the pharmacy. There were at least two people inside—a man and a woman.

A moment later, the clerk handed a slip of paper to the man behind him, who opened the door to the pharmacy and went inside. Errand Boy came out a few minutes later. The clerk looked at him. Errand Boy nodded once.

"Looks like we have what you want," the clerk said to the man holding the box. His gaze flicked to the box. Derrick couldn't see what was in the box, but he assumed there was food in it. "That's not enough to pay for what you want."

The man shook his head. "But it's...it's all I have."

The clerk smirked. "Not my problem." He looked past the man to the woman. "Next."

The woman took a step forward, but the man blocked her. "Wait!"

Looking bored, the clerk shifted his eyes to the man.

"My wife *needs* that medicine." Pleading filled the man's voice.

The clerk frowned. "Apparently not or you'd pay the full price."

The man's shoulders went back as he stood straighter. He set the box of food on the table. "This is a fair payment." He palmed his hips. "I *demand* that you give me that medicine."

The clerk's eyebrows rose, then he began to laugh. "You *demand?*" He shook his head. "The price has doubled." He grabbed the box of food and handed it to Errand Boy. "That's your deposit." One side of his mouth tugged up. "Non-refundable."

The man began to tremble. With rage or fear, Derrick didn't know. He couldn't see the man's face, only the back of him. The man's right hand slowly slid from his hip toward his back. That's when Derrick saw a bulge under his shirt. He was reaching for a gun.

Giving Matt a sideways look, Derrick subtly gestured with his head for them to move to the left. Matt took a step in that direction and Derrick followed. This caught the attention of Baldy and the other guard, who looked away from the irate customer.

"Where're you going?" Baldy shouted.

Everyone—except the irate customer—looked their way.

Holding the cans of food, Derrick held his hands up to show he meant no harm. At that moment, the irate customer shot the clerk in the head. The woman behind the irate customer screamed as the clerk slumped forward, his head hitting the table. Both guards and Errand Boy drew their weapons and began shooting at the man. He fell to the ground. The woman behind him screamed and screamed until her screams were silenced by several gunshots. Her bag of goods fell to the ground and cans of food tumbled across the sidewalk.

These guys were ruthless. Yeah, they'd shot back at the man who'd killed their clerk, but then they'd killed the woman. Not able to stand there and do nothing, Derrick dropped his cans of food and pulled his Glock from his holster. He aimed at the first guard, hitting him in chest. Matt drew his weapon as well and shot the other guard. Derrick shifted his aim to Errand Boy, who was now pointing his gun at Derrick. They both fired. A burning sensation tore across Derrick's neck, but Errand Boy collapsed to the ground.

The smell of gun powder hung in the air. A high-pitched ringing sounded in Derrick's ears. Ignoring the sound and keeping his eyes on the men who were down, he carefully made his way to the table. He and Matt checked the men for a pulse. He looked at Matt and shook his head. Matt did the same.

They were all dead.

"The people inside," Matt said with a look toward the glass doors.

Nodding, Derrick pressed his back to the wall beside the entrance, then looked at Matt, who nodded once. Matt pushed the door inward while at the same time Derrick leapt into the open doorway, leading with his gun. "Everyone down!"

"Don't shoot!" a woman shouted. "We're not armed!"

With his gaze scanning the darkened interior, Derrick

sized it up. A man wearing a white pharmacist's smock and a woman wearing a pale blue smock had their hands high in the air. No one else was in sight.

"Are you alone?" Derrick asked.

"Yes," the man said. His forehead creased. "What happened?"

Derrick motioned with his head toward the front of the store. "They're dead."

Relief washed across the man's face and his hands started to droop. Then his gaze went to the gun in Derrick's hand, which was still pointed at him. Fresh fear claimed his expression as his hands went back up. "What do you want?"

These people didn't seem to be a threat. Derrick lowered his weapon. "Put your hands down."

The man's shoulders sagged as he lowered his arms. The woman followed suit.

Derrick glanced toward Matt, who was clearing the space. He came back a moment later with a nod. Derrick holstered his Glock, then looked from the woman to the man. "What was going on here?"

Exhaling audibly, the woman shook her head. "Those men wouldn't let us leave."

The pharmacist nodded. "They said we worked for them now and if we tried to leave, they'd kill us." He paused a beat. "Who are you?"

"I'm Derrick and this is Matt."

The pharmacist nodded. "I'm Todd and this is Jenny." Todd looked between Derrick and Matt. "Why are you here?"

Derrick explained about Jeff and Doc.

Todd smiled. "Old Doc sent you, huh?" He laughed and shook his head.

Derrick didn't want to hang around any longer than necessary. "Yeah. Can you help us?"

"I can do more than that." Todd grinned. "If you'll help, we can bring the remaining meds to Doc."

That sounded like a good idea to Derrick. He glanced toward the dead men outside. "Should we be expecting any other members of their group to show up?"

Todd shook his head. "It was just the four of them."

"Good." He turned to Matt. "Wait here while I get the truck."

Matt agreed and Derrick turned to leave.

"Hold on," Jenny said.

Derrick swiveled back around. "What?"

She touched her neck. "Your neck's bleeding."

He'd forgotten about that. The adrenaline had masked the sting. "Doc can take a look at it."

She smiled. "Right."

At that, he strode out of the pharmacy to get his truck.

CHAPTER 22

Jessica

THE SOUND of Derrick's truck was music to Jessica's ears. From the moment they'd left, she'd been a nervous wreck. After all they'd been through that day, not knowing what was happening had been torture.

The kids stood with her under the branches of a large tree in Doc's yard. Chris and his family were nearby.

"Who's in the truck with them?" Dylan asked.

Jessica stared at the people in the back seat. A man and a woman. What was going on?

Derrick turned off the truck and Matt hopped out, a smile on his face as he came straight to Jessica. That was a good sign.

The man and woman, one wearing a white smock the other a blue smock, climbed out of the back seat.

"Who's that?" Jessica murmured when Matt gathered her in a hug.

Laughing as he released her, he said, "We brought a lot more than the antibiotics that Jeff needs."

"What?"

He quickly told them what had happened. Imagining the shootout ending with Matt or Derrick getting shot sent a cascade of terror winding its way through her. Then she saw the blood dripping from Derrick's neck.

"Are you okay?" she asked him.

He touched his neck with a frown. "I'll be fine." He pointed to his truck. "Let's get this stuff unloaded."

Everyone pitched in and in short order they had all the supplies stowed in a room in Doc's house, including the food, water, and other items that had been on the long table in front of the pharmacy.

"This is wonderful," Doc said as he looked over what they'd brought. "So wonderful."

The woman who'd come with them—she'd said her name was Jenny—stepped forward. "Doc, can you take a look at Derrick's neck?"

Doc turned to Derrick. "Yes. Come with me."

Derrick frowned again, but he followed Doc into his exam room. Jeff had been moved to one of the bedrooms and was resting on a mattress. Jessica went to talk to Emily, who hadn't left Jeff's side.

"Derrick and Matt got the antibiotics," she said with a smile as she pulled an empty chair next to Emily and sat down.

"I know," Emily said, her face bright. "I saw all the stuff you guys brought in. Doc started Jeff on a course the moment the antibiotics arrived."

"Good."

"Did they have much trouble getting it?"

Jessica tilted her head. "A bit." Then she repeated Matt's story.

Emily shook her head. "That's so crazy. And terrifying. I'm glad everyone's okay." She frowned. "Well, everyone in our group and the pharmacist and tech."

Jessica agreed. All the death and killing they'd seen was awful. Why did people have to do such terrible things?

She voiced her thoughts.

Emily looked at Jeff, who was sleeping peacefully, then back at Jessica. "I know. It's insane how people behave when law and order is gone. I guess everyone's true nature comes out. For better or worse."

What was her true nature? She'd shot that woman at the rest stop. Yes, it had only been in the foot, but still. She'd *shot* her.

Emily must have read her thoughts. "You had no choice, Jessica. You were protecting your daughter."

True as that was, she was still having a hard time with it. She faced Emily. "What about us? I mean, the rest of our group." She glanced at Jeff. "Jeff and Derrick. And...and Matt. They've killed people."

Emily shook her head, her expression sure. "Nope. That doesn't work for me. They weren't the aggressors. They weren't looking for trouble." She held up her hand and pointed to one finger. "Men were burning your house down." She touched another finger. "Those people shot at you. People you were trying to help." She touched a third finger and a fourth. "That man barreled onto the freeway and shot at Derrick. Those men at the rest stop shot first." Dropping her hands into her lap, she shook her head. "And from what you just told me, those men at the pharmacy were holding people hostage and extorting other people for medicine that wasn't theirs."

Hearing it all laid out like that assuaged Jessica's guilt to a great degree. "You're right." She smiled. "Thank you."

Jeff opened his eyes and looked at Emily. "Hey, baby."

"Hey. How are you feeling?"

Slowly, he pushed himself into a sitting position. "Better." He smiled at Jessica. "Is everyone waiting on me?"

"You and Derrick."

"What happened to Derrick?"

Jessica repeated the story again.

Jeff shook his head. "I should've been there."

Emily rolled her eyes. "They were getting the meds for you, goofball."

Jeff chuckled.

Jessica stood. "I'm going to check on Derrick."

Nodding, Jeff said. "Great. We can get going as soon as he's good to go."

Jessica looked at Emily to see if she would object, but she seemed just as eager to get going as Jeff was. Jessica nodded. "Will do."

She left the room and went to the exam room. Derrick was sitting on the table, all alone, a gauze bandage on his neck.

"How're you doing?"

He smirked. "I'll be fine. It's just a flesh wound."

"Where's Doc?"

Now Derrick laughed. "Went to get me some antibiotics."

Grinning, Jessica said, "Good thing you brought back extra."

He laughed. "How's Jeff doing?"

"Okay, I guess. He wants to leave as soon as possible."

Derrick nodded. "Yeah. We should hit the road. Todd and Jenny said no one else was involved in the pharmacy thing, but you never know."

She shook her head. "We just leave a trail of enemies in our wake, don't we?"

One side of his mouth quirked up. "Not all enemies."

She pictured Doc and how happy he'd been to receive the supplies. Not to mention Todd and Jenny being freed. Yeah, not everyone was bad news.

"Would you tell everyone to get ready to go?" Derrick asked.

"Sure." She went outside and let the rest of the group know that both Derrick and Jeff wanted to head out as soon as possible.

CHAPTER 23

Chris

ONCE THEY WERE BACK on I-80 heading west, Chris breathed a sigh of relief. Waiting for Derrick and Matt to come back from the pharmacy had been difficult. He would have preferred to go with them, but leaving Amy and the boys unprotected wasn't something he was willing to do. Not when their group was traveling and didn't know the people in the area. Too risky. On the positive side, the break had been nice for the kids. Jacob and Aaron had been able to stretch their legs and work off some of their boundless energy.

"I like Jessica," Amy said from the passenger seat.

"Yeah. She and Matt are good people."

Sagebrush stretched off into the distance all around them. Occasionally a car or truck drove past heading the other direction. Every time a vehicle approached, Chris braced himself for something bad to happen, but nothing did. He tried to relax, but it was difficult. Not when danger could be around the next bend.

"Believe it or not," Amy said, "I'm glad you convinced me that we should leave our house and go to California."

Chris looked at her in surprise. "Really?"

She smiled. "Yes, really."

"What made you change your mind? The shootout at the rest stop or the tale of Derrick and Matt's trip to the pharmacy?"

That earned him a laugh. "Both and neither."

Baffled, he shifted his gaze to her. "What?"

"All the scary things that happened today underscored to me what people are willing to do when they're desperate. With all those gang members moving into our neighborhood, it wouldn't have been safe to stay there." She paused. "I know it's dangerous out here, but once we reach Emily's aunt and uncle's farm, we'll be safe. Right?"

Chris wanted to reassure her that once they reached their destination all would be well, but he had no clue if that was true, no idea what they would find when they got there. Regardless, after everything that had happened in their old neighborhood, it wouldn't be any safer there than being on the road. They'd had no choice but to leave.

"Yeah," he finally said with a smile he hoped was reassuring. What else could he say? Besides, he didn't want to douse Amy's hope. They all needed hope. It's what kept them going.

The walkie sitting on the dashboard squawked and Derrick's voice came over the line. "Something's going on up ahead on the right shoulder. Show caution. Over."

Chris picked up the walkie. "Copy." He looked at Amy.

The optimism she'd shown seconds before melted from her face. Eyes tight with worry, she asked, "Can you see anything?"

The entire group was traveling in the right lane, well under the speed limit to avoid hitting any obstacles that were sometimes in the road. Chris and Amy were the last car in the caravan. One by one, the three vehicles in front of them moved to the left lane, clearing Chris's view of what was up ahead.

A small car was parked on the shoulder. Standing beside it were a man and a woman having what appeared to be an argument. The man held a little girl who couldn't have been more than two-years-old. She was crying hysterically, her arms reaching for the woman. The woman's back was to Chris, but her shoulders shook and her arms were outstretched like she wanted the child.

The man glanced at the approaching caravan and, without warning, set the little girl down. He pointed her toward the road and gently pushed her. The little girl began to toddle forward, right into the path of the caravan. The woman moved as if to get the girl, but the man grabbed her by the arm, stopping her.

Their caravan slowed dramatically, obviously to avoid hitting the little girl. Though Derrick, Matt, and Emily had pulled into the left lane, Chris straddled the line dividing the two lanes so his view of what was happening wouldn't be obstructed.

Inching forward, Derrick's truck drew closer, although he was still about forty feet away from the child. Chris watched with mounting horror as the little girl blithely strolled into Derrick's path.

"Look out!" Amy shouted as if Derrick could hear her.

Chris slammed on his brakes. Good thing, because Derrick had slammed on his, causing a chain reaction of brakes being pressed. Emily nearly crashed into the RV in front of her. She probably hadn't been able to see what was going on. Fortunately, she'd kept a decent distance behind the RV.

Chris shifted his gaze to the couple. The man still held the woman by the arm. Clearly outraged, the woman lifted her free arm and slapped the man across the face. He released her arm, but then he slammed his fist into her gut. She doubled over and fell to the asphalt.

This guy was too much. First sending a baby into the road when a truck was coming, and then hitting the woman. If there was one thing Chris wouldn't tolerate, it was a man hitting a woman. He shut off the engine and opened his door.

"Where are you going?" Amy asked, her voice laced with fear.

Chris turned to her with a grimace. "I have to do something. That guy has to be stopped."

Her forehead creased. "But what if he's dangerous?"

He looked toward the couple. The woman was still on the ground while the man stood with his hands on his hips, staring at her with a murderous glare. That's when Chris saw Derrick and Matt running toward them. Chris glanced at Amy one last time before jumping out of the truck and hurrying to the join the conflict, reaching it moments after Derrick and Matt. Jessica had also gotten out, picking up the little girl.

"What's going on here?" Derrick asked.

Matt knelt on the asphalt beside the woman.

The man—six feet tall and muscular—held his elbows wide from his body with his chest thrust out. "Mind your own business."

Chris had seen enough. He stepped toward the man. "No can do. Hitting a woman is not acceptable."

The man turned his gaze on Chris. "Says who?" A grin split his face as he looked at each of them in turn. "You three?"

"Stop it, Alex," the woman said, then she tried to stand. Matt put an arm around her to help her up.

Alex shoved Matt, hard. "Don't touch her!"

Matt fell backwards with a grunt, nearly hitting his head on the asphalt.

Without hesitation, Chris plowed in to Alex. The guy was built like a tree trunk. Maybe this hadn't been such a good idea. They crashed to the ground. Chris landed on top of Alex, who bellowed like an angry bull whose territory had been invaded.

Chris got in a few punches, but this guy was strong, and when he slammed a fist into Chris's kidney, Chris fell back. He needed a moment to recover, but the guy didn't give him one, ramming into Chris.

A little help?

Chris caught Derrick's eye, and a moment later Derrick joined the fray. Between the two of them they managed to subdue Alex, pinning him face down against the rough asphalt. Derrick held Alex's arms behind his back at an awkward angle, keeping him immobilized.

"Alex!" the woman cried as she rushed to his side and tried to push Derrick off of him. "Don't hurt him!" The woman was tiny—couldn't have been much over five feet tall and maybe a hundred pounds. Her efforts had no effect.

Ignoring her, Chris patted Alex down to make sure he

wasn't armed. Just a pocket knife, which Chris tucked in his own pocket.

"Let him go!" the woman yelled, her voice frantic.

What was wrong with her? Chris stood and looked at her in disbelief. "He hit you."

Tears shimmered in her blue eyes. "But I need him. I...I can't make it out here by myself."

Was this what this world had come to? A woman would rather be with a man who hurt her—who endangered her child—than be on her own?

Chris glanced at Alex. "Is he your husband?"

She shook her head.

"Boyfriend?"

She shook her head again.

Chris tilted his head and narrowed his eyes. "The father of the child?" Which he found hard to fathom, since the man had sent the girl into the path of an oncoming truck.

"No."

This was getting stranger by the second. "How long have you known him?"

"A...a week."

Jessica stepped up beside Chris. "What's your name?"

The woman, who looked so young and vulnerable, turned to Jessica. "Paisley."

Jessica held the toddler up. "And this little cutie?"

Paisley smiled. "That's Serena." She took Serena from Jessica. The child wrapped her arms around Paisley's neck and laid her head on Paisley's shoulder. "It's okay now, baby," Paisley murmured.

It wasn't though, was it? Not if she was going to stay with a violent man she'd met the week before.

A crazy thought jumped into Chris's mind. *Bring her with us.* He shook his head to dislodge it, but it wouldn't go away. *Bring her with us.*

By this time, Matt had gotten a rope out of his RV and had bound Alex's hands and feet and put a wide piece of duct tape across the man's mouth.

Chris walked over to Derrick. "We need to talk."

CHAPTER 24

Derrick

DERRICK COULDN'T BELIEVE what Chris was proposing. Bring the woman and child with them? What was he thinking? Why would they want to add two more mouths to feed? And mouths belonging to people who wouldn't add anything to their group? It made no sense.

"I don't know," Derrick said as he and Chris stood off to the side. He motioned for Matt and Jessica to join them.

"Let me get Amy and Emily," Jessica said.

A short time later all the adults—except Jeff, who was sleeping in the truck—huddled together to discuss Chris's suggestion. Derrick kept a sharp eye on Alex, who glared at them. Brooke and Kayla had brought Cleo over to show Serena, who giggled with delight at the antics of the rambunctious German shepherd.

She and Paisley were a good distance away from Alex, with Paisley glancing nervously at Alex, like she was scared of what he would do once she was left alone with him. That didn't sit well with Derrick.

Shoving down the feeling, he focused on the conversation.

"She's all alone," Chris said. "She and her kid."

Well of course Chris would say that. He had two little kids himself. And a wife. He probably saw Paisley and Serena as stand-ins for his family and imagined what it would be like for them if they were on their own. "Don't be so sentimental, Chris. They're dead weight."

Jessica's mouth fell open as she looked at him. "Really, Derrick?"

Now he felt like a jerk. Was he wrong to think that way? He looked at the others to gauge their feelings, stopping on Matt.

Matt stared back. "We have plenty of food. Anyway, shouldn't we get to the farm soon? Like, by tomorrow?"

"In normal times," Emily began, "it takes us about twelve hours. Sometimes longer, depending on how often we stop."

She was making his point for him. "So, in normal times we should be there in a couple of hours. Instead, we're not even halfway there." They all looked at him. Why did he always have to be the bad guy, the one who pointed out logic? "Just sayin' it might take longer than you expect. Which means we can't assume anything."

Matt gazed at him steadily. "We have enough, Derrick."

"Look at her," Amy said. "I don't think she's capable of eating much. And if her little girl is anything like Aaron, she won't eat much either."

Clearly, no one was on his side. He threw his hands up. "Fine. If you all want to be responsible for some woman and her kid, be my guest."

"Where's she going to ride?" Emily asked. "I mean, Jeff's stretched out on the back seat, so I don't think I can fit her and her daughter in our truck."

Not meeting the eyes of anyone, Derrick fiddled with the knife in his pocket. He knew what they were thinking. She and the kid should ride with him. He was all alone in his truck. He had plenty of room, blah blah blah. But no, he wasn't about to offer. He was the only one who didn't want them to come. He wasn't about to be their chauffeur.

"They can ride with us," Amy said.

Derrick lifted his eyes to look at Chris, who, to Derrick's surprise, looked fine with Amy's idea. Well, their SUV could seat seven.

"That works," Chris said.

"Just one problem," Emily said. "What if she doesn't want to come with us?"

That wouldn't be a problem at all. No. That would *solve* the problem.

Derrick kept his thoughts to himself.

"I'll ask her," Jessica said, then she trotted right over to the woman.

Derrick couldn't hear their conversation, but he watched as Jessica presented the idea. Paisley's eyebrows shot up, then her eyes went to the group, stopping on each person as if to see if they meant it. When her eyes met Derrick's, he glanced away. He'd never been great at hiding his feelings.

A couple of seconds later he looked at Paisley again. She was hugging her daughter and talking excitedly to her. Great. Clearly, that meant she was coming.

Jessica waved everyone over. While the rest of the group helped Paisley move her things from her car to Chris and

Amy's, including a car seat, Derrick went over to Alex to have a little chat. He tore the duct tape from the man's mouth, which immediately released a round of vigorous swearing.

"Shut up," Derrick growled, "or I'll put it back on that ugly face of yours."

Alex quieted down.

"Looks like you're on your own."

Several emotions washed across Alex's face, then he looked in the direction of Paisley before shifting his eyes to Derrick. "Good riddance to her."

Derrick hoped he was saying that out of spite and not because he was really glad to be rid of her.

Because now she was their problem.

CHAPTER 25

Chris

CHRIS HALF-LISTENED as Amy and Paisley chatted comfortably. They'd had to rearrange a few things to make room for the two additional passengers, but they'd made it work. Chris was still kind of astonished that he'd insisted on bringing these two with them. They'd passed many people on this journey, but he'd never felt the desire to invite any of them along. So, what was different this time?

With no idea, he shoved aside the question and focused on driving.

"How did you end up with Alex?" Amy asked.

Chris glanced in the rearview mirror to see Paisley's reaction. She reached out and touched Serena, who was sleeping in her car seat beside her. "It's a long story."

"I don't mind." Amy chuckled. "I don't have anything else to do."

"Okay. Well, Serena and I were living in Idaho with my

parents, but then…" She went quiet for a moment. "They got sick and…they died."

"I'm so sorry," Amy said, her voice gentle.

"Thanks. It was…it was hard." She softly sighed. "Anyway, I just, I couldn't stay there after that, so I packed up Serena and left."

Chris found himself getting caught up in her story. "Where were you headed?"

She laughed. "That's the dumb thing. I had no idea where to go. I just…went."

Was she normally so impulsive? Or had the trauma of losing her parents sent her over the edge? No matter. She was part of their group now.

"What happened then?" Amy asked.

"Like an idiot, I ran out of gas. In the middle of nowhere. In the middle of the night."

"That must have been terrifying," Amy said. "I mean, now that things are so crazy."

"It was. Which is why when Alex came along and offered to help, I accepted. I mean, he seemed like a nice guy at first. And he actually did help me a lot. But sometimes he…" Her words trailed off.

Chris glanced at her again, then thought about the way Alex had put Serena in extreme danger and had kept Paisley from protecting her daughter. Not to mention punching her in the stomach. The man was clearly evil.

"Never mind," Amy said. "I'm just glad we came along when we did."

"Me too." Earnest gratitude filled Paisley's voice.

They drove in silence for a good ten minutes before Derrick's voice came over the walkie.

"Pulling off up ahead. Over."

Two minutes later their convoy had pulled well off of the shoulder into the grassy area to the right of the road. Unsure of why Derrick had stopped, Chris turned too Amy. "Wait here while I see what's going on."

Jogging over to where Derrick, Matt, Jessica, and Emily were gathering, Chris let his gaze sweep the surrounding area. Nothing was in sight. Just short grass and sagebrush.

"What's going on?" he asked as he joined the group.

"We're about halfway to the farm," Derrick said. "Feels like it's time to stop for the day."

They'd been on the road all day, and after everything they'd been through, Chris didn't disagree.

"There's no way we'll make it to the farm today," Derrick said. "And I want to be fresh when we pass through Reno."

"How far is Reno from here?" Matt asked.

"Less than two hundred miles." One side of Derrick's mouth quirked up. "I don't know about you guys, but I'm ready for a break. A long break."

Chris nodded. It had been a crazy day, and if the next day was anything like it, they would need the rest. He glanced around. "Where do you want to set up camp?"

Derrick shrugged. "This place seems as good a place as any. We'll need to take turns keeping watch tonight, but if we circle our vehicles and camp in the middle of the circle, we should be safe."

"Circle the wagons," Chris said with a grin. "I like it."

Derrick smiled. "Exactly." He paused a beat. "How's it going with the new people?"

Lifting his shoulders in a shrug, Chris said, "Fine. She seems legit."

"What's her story?"

Chris repeated what Paisley had shared—which wasn't a whole lot, really.

Derrick nodded, then he looked at all of them. "Let's get set up."

After a bit of maneuvering, they formed a rough circle with their vehicles. Matt and Emily left their trailers hitched to their trucks. Everyone gathered in the interior of the circle, including Jeff, who said he was feeling better.

Chris helped Derrick and Matt set up the two large tents that had been stashed in Jeff and Emily's small utility trailer, then they laid out sleeping bags.

Chris was a bit concerned about how well he and Amy would sleep that night, what with the kids not sleeping in their beds like they were used to. Regardless, they would all have to adjust to sleeping wherever they were. He doubted they would ever return to their home. Instead, home would be wherever they were, not a structure where they had their stuff.

CHAPTER 26

Jessica

JESSICA TURNED AWAY from the tents and gazed at the RV. She bit her lip, then swiveled to face the others. It didn't seem fair that she and her family would sleep in such comfort while the rest of them slept on the ground. "We can fit a few people in the RV. On the couch and the floor."

Everyone turned to look at her.

"I'll probably sleep under the stars," Derrick said with a smirk before going back to checking the tent cords tethered to the hard-packed dirt.

Jessica looked at Amy and Paisley, who were keeping a close eye on their children. Amy regarded Chris, her eyebrows raised in question.

"The kids might sleep better indoors," he said.

Amy smiled at Jessica. "If you're sure you have room."

"I'll sleep in a tent," Chris added.

Jessica smiled at Amy. "We'll make it work."

Amy glanced at Paisley before meeting Jessica's gaze with a meaningful expression.

Jessica didn't know this new person. Didn't have the history she had with the rest of the group. Could Paisley be trusted? Maybe putting out the open invitation to sleep in the RV had been a mistake.

"That would be wonderful," Paisley said, putting an end to Jessica's hope that maybe she would decline the offer. "Thank you so much."

The woman seemed sincere. And she had a little girl for heaven's sake. Besides, Jessica had wanted the chance to help someone. Here was her chance. Of course she would welcome her into their RV. At least for the night. She smiled, and it wasn't all forced. "You're welcome."

Once that was settled, Jessica had Dylan and the girls set up the folding table they kept in the RV's basement before putting their red-checked tablecloth on it and taking out a stack of paper plates. Matt set up his Camp Chef stove and used some water from their fresh water tank to fill a large pot before turning on the flame to boil the water.

Matt took out one of the buckets of freeze-dried food and read off of the front. "We've got cheesy lasagna, creamy pasta, chili mac, and savory stroganoff." He smiled at the assembled group. "Take your pick."

To her surprise, Jessica's mouth watered at the prospect of any one of those choices. They'd been trying to conserve their food, so she hadn't eaten much that day. Since all the madness had begun two weeks earlier, she'd lost at least ten pounds— weight she'd been trying to get off for a while before the pandemic hit. This wasn't the way she'd planned on losing weight, but The Apocalypse Diet was the only one that had worked so far.

Holding back a chuckle, she helped get the meal ready, then sat down with her plate of food. Paisley sat across from her.

"Are you sure you're okay with Serena and me sleeping in your RV? I mean, you just met me today." She glanced at the tents. "We'd be fine in a tent." She laughed. "It wouldn't be much different from sleeping in the car, which is what I've been doing for days now."

The poor woman had been under a real hardship. And now she was giving Jessica an out. "No," Jessica said. "I insist that you sleep in the RV."

Tears sprang into Paisley's eyes. She looked down at her lap for a moment, then met Jessica's gaze. "Thank you. Truly."

Feeling silly for having doubts earlier, Jessica let the warmth of knowing she was helping out someone who really needed it wash over her.

After everyone ate, they cleaned up—which didn't take long as almost everything was disposable. How long would their paper plates hold out? Eventually they'd run out and then what would they do? She and Matt had eight real plates, but with water such a precious commodity, they didn't want to have to use it to do dishes.

"We'll set up the latrine back there," Derrick said, pointing to a place a fair distance behind their camp. He gestured with his chin toward Matt and Dylan. "I could use some help setting it up."

At the look of disgust on Dylan's face, Jessica held back a laugh. "It's just dirt right now, Dylan."

An embarrassed smile curved his lips. "I know."

Off they went, and while they were gone, the rest of the group pulled up camp chairs to create a large circle. Cleo curled up on the ground between Brooke and Kayla. Jessica smiled at the sight.

"Too bad there's nothing to burn around here," Jeff said. Emily had wrapped a warm blanket around him. Besides looking a bit pale, he seemed to be doing better than he had been earlier that day.

"Yes," Emily said from beside him. "A campfire would be perfect right about now."

Jessica agreed. As the sun began to descend toward the horizon, she felt a definite chill in air. It was still April, after all.

Matt, Dylan, and Derrick joined them a short time later.

"Okay," Emily said with a smirk as she stood, "I'll try out that latrine."

Everyone laughed. When she got back—and after several more people had put the latrine to use—they began talking about their plans for the next day.

"We'll leave at first light," Derrick said.

Heads nodded in agreement.

"Do you think we'll make it to the farm tomorrow?" Amy asked.

"With any luck we will," Jeff said.

Matt laughed. "There's the catch. Our luck hasn't been the best."

"Oh, I don't know about that," Jeff replied. "I mean, we *are* all still alive."

They all chuckled.

Jessica deeply hoped they would get there the next day.

She was beyond ready to be done with this road trip and settled in to their new place where she assumed they'd be safe.

"Hold on a sec," Paisley said, looking confused. Everyone looked her way. "If you don't mind me asking, what farm?"

"Of course you can ask," Emily said, clearly having no issue with the newcomer joining them at her aunt and uncle's farm. "My aunt and uncle have a farm in the San Joaquin Valley in California. That's where we're headed."

Paisley's eyebrows rose. "That sounds awesome. I mean, I grew up on a farm, so..." She let her words trail off.

CHAPTER 27

Derrick

MAYBE PAISLEY WOULDN'T BE dead weight after all. At least once they got to this farm they were headed to.

Trying to be subtle, Derrick scrutinized Paisley a little more closely. She didn't look like she could lift more than thirty pounds. And with her flowing blonde hair, she looked more like a flighty actress than a farm girl.

Ah well. They would reach the farm soon and then Emily's aunt and uncle could decide if she—or any of them—were welcome. He pushed aside the thought. They had plenty to deal with before they got to that point.

Once the sun set, people started heading off to bed. Derrick had volunteered to take first watch, so he stood and began patrolling the outer perimeter of their circle. Eventually, the night became pitch black. Tilting his head back, he gazed at the stars. They were absolutely brilliant. He took a moment to admire the Milky Way.

With his eyes adjusted to the dark night, he peered into

the distance as he strode toward I-80. No cars could be seen in either direction. He turned his back to the road and looked toward their camp, gauging how visible it would be in the dark. Probably not visible at all until a car's headlights swept across it. But by then the car would have passed and whoever was on watch would be aware of the vehicle and able to watch for it to possibly backtrack.

It seemed highly unlikely that anyone would manage to sneak up on them. Still, Derrick made a slow circuit around the perimeter of the camp again, checking out the approach to the camp from the wild area to the north. It would be nearly impossible to see anyone coming from that direction, but any intruder would have to be on foot as there was nothing in that direction but miles and miles of sagebrush. Nothing to hide behind.

During his three-hour watch, not one car passed by, and when Chris came out to relieve him, Derrick was more than ready to get some sleep.

"Wake me up if you see anything," he said to Chris, who nodded his agreement.

Staying fully dressed, including wearing his shoes, Derrick laid his sleeping bag in the bed of his truck and stretched out on top. With his hands behind his head, he gazed at the stars, soaking in the beauty of the night sky. It didn't take long for him to drift off, but he woke abruptly when he heard a shout. It took a second for him to orient himself to where he was, but the moment he did, he sat up, holding his gun in the low ready position, his eyes probing the darkness around him. From the bed of his truck, he could see the interior of the circle as well as a good portion of the area outside of the circle.

That's when he saw a pair of men crossing the eastbound lanes of I-80, coming toward their camp.

"I said to stop!" Matt shouted.

If Matt was on watch it had to be somewhere between three and six in the morning. Derrick slid out of the bed of his truck and hustled over to Matt, softly calling out to him so he wouldn't turn and shoot him by mistake. Matt acknowledged Derrick's approach, then turned his attention back to the men, who had halted in the grassy area between the east and westbound lanes of I-80.

Derrick looked behind him to see if Chris had woken. Sure enough, Chris gave Derrick a brief wave as he trotted to the other side of the circle, obviously to make sure no one was sneaking up on that side while Derrick and Matt were distracted. Derrick waved back.

"What do you want?" Matt called to the men, his gun pointed at them. Derrick aimed his Glock at the men as well.

The two men appeared to be having a brief conversation, which made Derrick uneasy. "Move along," Derrick called out. "You're not welcome here."

The men stopped talking and faced them. "We just want something to eat. Do you have any to spare?"

Shaking his head and sighing, Derrick glanced at Matt, who looked just as torn as he felt. They had a good amount, but they couldn't feed the world. Besides, for all Derrick knew, these men had a dozen others waiting to rush in and take all they had. Why confirm for them that their group had supplies worth taking?

"Can't help you," Derrick called out. "Now, move along."

The men stood where they were, speaking to each other in voices Derrick couldn't hear. They slowly began walking forward, ignoring Derrick's command to leave. Derrick shifted the aim of his Glock to the right of the men and squeezed the trigger. The blast of the gun shattered the quiet night air. The men threw their hands up, freezing in place.

Derrick brought his aim back to the man on the right. "I'm not going to tell you again!"

With their hands in the air, the men spun around, then they dropped their arms to their sides and took off running, disappearing into the darkness.

Exhaling in relief that they hadn't had to shoot anyone, Derrick holstered his gun and turned to Matt with a frown.

Matt tucked his gun into his waistband and glanced at his watch. "Sun will be rising soon."

"Good. I don't think I could go back to sleep now." Not with the adrenaline pumping through his veins.

Matt chuckled. "Never a dull moment."

Despite himself, Derrick grinned. "Nope."

Chris jogged over to meet them. "They must have been alone. There's nothing happening to the north."

Derrick nodded. "Good." He pursed his lips. "Might as well get breakfast going."

Matt smiled. "I'll get the water boiling."

Forty-five minutes later, their group had eaten and loaded up their gear.

Derrick spread out a map on the open tailgate of his truck while everyone gathered around. "The next town we'll pass through is Winnemucca." He pointed to it on the map. "It's not large, but it's big enough that we need to be on our guard. And it's the halfway point to our destination." Derrick looked at the others. "As time goes on, people are only going to get more desperate. We need to be ready for anything."

Looking grim, they nodded.

Derrick folded up the map and closed the gate on his truck. "All right. Let's head out."

As he led the way back onto I-80, Derrick hoped they'd be able to handle whatever they were going to face that day.

CHAPTER 28

Matt

As MATT FOLLOWED Derrick's truck, he silently said a prayer of thanks that they'd made it as far as they had and that he and his family were part of such a strong and smart group. If he and his family had had to make this trip on their own, there's no way they would have survived this long unscathed. Not only because he didn't have the experience, but even more, because he wouldn't have been able to do it alone. If Derrick hadn't come out that morning to back him up when those men had appeared out of the desert, it would have ended differently. Why would two men listen to one man? Especially when they were desperate? Of course, Matt could have shot them both—although, let's be honest, he wasn't *that* great a shot. But he wanted to keep the body count to a minimum.

"What are you thinking about?" Jessica asked as she rested her hand on his arm.

He smiled at her. "Just how lucky we are to be part of this group."

She nodded as a soft smile curved her lips. "I couldn't agree more." She chuckled. "And I like the new girl. Paisley?" She paused. "You know, I'd been hesitant to let her spend the night in the RV with us, but she was delightful."

"Don't forget how cute her baby is," Kayla said from the back seat.

Jessica laughed. "Yes, Serena is definitely adorable."

They drove on, eventually entering Winnemucca. On edge as they drove, Matt was on high alert for trouble. The Interstate was on the outskirts of town, and much to Matt's relief, they passed through without incident.

After they'd driven for another two hours, Derrick's voice came over the walkie. "Let's stop up ahead for a short break."

"Thank goodness," Jessica said.

Smiling, Matt picked up the walkie. "Copy that."

Their caravan pulled onto the right shoulder, although they were still partially on the road, which didn't matter as traffic was non-existent. Everyone jumped out of the truck, including Cleo, who immediately began sniffing everything in the immediate vicinity.

Matt intertwined his fingers with Jessica's before they walked together to meet up with the rest of their group, who were gathering beside Jeff and Emily's truck.

Though Jeff had seemed to be doing well when they'd left that morning, Matt was still concerned about him. They needed him—they needed every member of their group, but they especially needed Jeff. Not only was he courageous, he was a no-nonsense kind of man. In this insane world, their group would be much safer with him whole and healthy.

Jeff was just getting out of the truck when Matt and Jessica got there. He looked good to Matt, but what did he know? He was a computer programmer—*had been* a computer programmer—not a medical specialist.

Matt walked up to Jeff. "How're you doing?"

"I'm ready to drive." He smirked at Emily. "But Em won't let me. Insists I need to rest."

She smiled warmly at him. "You can drive after Reno."

He frowned. "Uh-huh."

This time she smirked. "Besides, I need you in the shotgun seat to ward off the bad guys."

This made everyone laugh. But only because it was so tragically true. They all needed to keep their guns loaded and within reach at all times. Matt reached behind him to reassure himself that his gun was in his waistband.

"Fifteen minute break," Derrick said, bringing them all back to reality, "then back on the road."

"How far are we from Reno?" Chris asked.

Reno's population before the pandemic had been close to two hundred and fifty thousand. Who knew how many people were left now? Then again, it only took a small group of desperate people to cause a huge problem.

Derrick pulled his map out of his back pocket and spread it out on the hood of Jeff and Emily's truck. He pointed to a spot east of Reno. "We're about here, so about 60 miles from Reno."

No one said anything, but Matt was sure they were all thinking the same thing: What problems would they face as they passed through Reno, Nevada?

The fifteen minutes passed in a flash, and as they drove ever westward, Matt pictured their destination. Or at least what he hoped he would find once they got there. Lush, green fields with rows and rows of fresh vegetables ripe for the eating. White and black cows calling out to be milked. Plump chickens producing baskets-full of fresh eggs daily. Plenty of space for the kids to run around. A spacious house with room for all—including a private bedroom for him and Jessica. And finally, an easily protected perimeter to keep out anyone who would do them harm.

All of that was worth risking their lives to reach.

Matt looked to his left and saw the Truckee River. On the right was a sign with the logos of several gas stations—something that in the past he would potentially take advantage of. Now, though, those gas stations were most certainly dry.

As they approached Sparks, which was just east of Reno, an overpass came into view. Automatically lifting his gaze to the elevated road, Matt felt his heart speed up. Was there a sniper up there just waiting to take him and his family out?

He couldn't see anyone, and once they passed underneath without anyone shooting at them, he softly exhaled.

"So far so good," Jessica murmured beside him.

So, she was just as on edge as he was. He didn't know why that should surprise him. She'd experienced most of the same things he had, although he was grateful he'd managed to spare her some of it.

"We're going to make it," he said, as much to reassure himself as her.

She smiled at him, her eyes tight with worry.

They passed under another overpass. No shooting. A shopping center was on their right. The parking lots were deserted like it was a holiday. Only it wasn't. It felt eerie and unsettling. Like someone could suddenly appear out of nowhere and that someone would not have good intentions.

They passed a sign with the logos of several fast food joints. The thought of eating at any one of those places made Matt's mouth water, but restaurants were now a remnant of the past. Would they ever return? He hoped so, but with the number of people severely depleted, it would be a long time before life could return to normal—if it ever did.

They entered the Reno city limits, staying in the left lane of the Interstate. An occasional car passed them heading east, and they passed a car heading west here and there. No one seemed to pay attention to them, which was exactly how Matt wanted it.

A sign over the freeway directed them to stay in their lane if they wanted to go toward Sacramento, which was the capitol of California.

They were getting closer.

CHAPTER 29

Derrick

THEY'D MADE it across Reno, but as they approached the western edge, a large hand-lettered sign caught Derrick's eye. *GAS AVAILABLE*

He picked up the walkie. "Anyone need to top off their tanks?"

Jeff and Chris said they wanted to.

Derrick wanted to as well. If they filled up here, they would have enough fuel to finish the trip without stopping again.

The four vehicles exited I-80 and drove to the gas station, which was clearly visible. No one else was gassing up, but that was fine with Derrick. The fewer people around, the better.

They pulled in to the station, each of them stopping beside a pump. A man came hustling out, a wide grin on his bearded face.

"Howdy! Need some gas, do you?"

Derrick had already gotten out of his truck. Matt, Chris, and Jeff joined him.

The man's name was stenciled on the pocket of his shirt. Everett. Was that really his name or had he taken the shirt from someone else? No matter. He was the one who controlled the pumps.

"How much you charging?" Derrick asked.

Everett's smile grew. "Doing it in trade. Cash does me no good."

The man wasn't an idiot. Derrick had to give him that. "What do you need?"

He chuckled. "Lots of things, but food and weapons carry the most value."

No way would they give up any weapons. "We'll trade a can of food per three gallons of gas." Between the four of them, they'd need around sixty gallons. That would be twenty cans of food.

Everett laughed. "Not even close, my friend."

"Do you even have that much fuel?" Jeff asked, his deep voice booming.

Derrick was glad to have him back in action.

Everett shot his gaze to Jeff, who towered over him. "I have plenty of fuel, sir. The question is, do you have the goods to trade?"

Jeff glowered. "We have one can of food per three gallons."

Everett stared at Jeff, clearly not about to back down. "Where y'all headed?"

Derrick didn't like his nosy question. "Why?"

Everett glanced toward the west, then turned back to face them. "If you're heading into California, might be worth your while to save your food and instead trade your weapons for fuel."

Crossing his arms over his chest, Derrick sighed heavily. "Now, why would we want to do that?"

A smirky smile curved Everett's lips. "They won't let you bring any guns across the border. They're confiscating all of 'em. Even from the people already in California."

Sudden alarm pierced Derrick. They needed their weapons. Not having them would leave them wide open to attack.

"Oh, hell no," Jeff said.

"You're kidding," Chris said, his body rigid.

Everett looked at Chris. "'Fraid not. They'll search your rig from top to bottom." He shook his head like he didn't agree with it either. "This world's gone barking mad."

That was the understatement of the year.

Derrick needed to know more. "Who's taking the guns?"

Everett turned to him. "State government. On the orders of the acting governor."

Chris shook his head. "Did the governor give a reason?"

This brought a smile to Everett's face. "Yeah. Claims it's for the protection of all. You know, if fewer people have guns, fewer people will be killed by guns."

Shaking his head in disgust, Derrick clenched his jaw. Some politician—guarded by armed men, no doubt—thought it was a good idea to disarm law-abiding citizens. That way only criminals would be armed. Just perfect.

"Lets not forget," Jeff said, "if the people are disarmed, the government can more easily control them."

Derrick sighed. "Exactly." Trying not to let his frustration get to him, he faced Everett. "Will you take one can for three gallons or not?"

Everett chewed on his lower lip as he stared at Derrick. "Two cans for three gallons. That's my final offer."

Jaw clenched, Derrick shifted his eyes to the others, stopping on Matt. He had the most food. And with his auxiliary tank, he probably didn't even need any fuel. Still, Matt gave a nearly imperceptible nod.

Derrick swiveled to Everett. "Deal."

A wide smile flashed across Everett's face. "How many gallons you think you'll need?"

"Forty-five of unleaded." He glanced at Matt.

Matt nodded. "Fifteen of diesel."

Everett's smile never dimmed. "That's forty cans. I'll need a deposit of half before you start pumpin'."

Derrick couldn't blame him, but he was still irritated. And he didn't fully trust the man. "How do we know you have enough fuel?"

Now he looked offended. "Like I said before, I have enough."

Derrick stared at him a moment. "Tell you what. We'll get the cans out, but we'll only hand them over as the fuel goes in our tanks."

Everett seemed to think that over. "If we're gonna do that, then we only fill one vehicle at a time."

"Fair enough." Derrick turned to the others.

Jeff grinned. "Line up in formation?"

Derrick had to chuckle. "Yep."

In short order, they'd all lined up with Derrick in the lead, then Matt, Jeff, and Chris. They took out a case of green beans and set it on the ground beside the pump. Then

Derrick started pumping. Every time they hit three gallons, he handed two cans to Everett. It took a while to fill all four vehicles, but when they were done, each of them had a full tank.

When they were back on the road, Derrick looked for a good place to pull over. One where they were less likely to be observed. He passed the off-ramp for a casino at Exit 2. Two miles from the California border.

He picked up the walkie. "Pulling over up ahead. Over."

The others acknowledged him, and when Exit 1 appeared, he pulled off, driving to a parking area near an abandoned building. Once everyone was stopped, he asked Chris to help him clear the building while Matt and Jeff kept watch.

It didn't take long to verify that no one was around, and once he and Chris had completed that task, they met up with Matt and Jeff. The rest of their group joined them.

"What's the plan?" Emily asked. "Jeff told me they're confiscating guns at the border." Her forehead furrowed. "We're not going to give up our weapons, are we?" A laugh erupted from her lips as she glanced at Jeff. "Never mind. I know the answer to that."

Derrick looked at Jeff, who wore a deep scowl.

"Of course not," Derrick said in reply.

"Then what are we going to do?" Jessica asked.

He looked at all of their faces. They were looking to him to lead them, to get them through this. Just like they'd been looking to him to lead them since they'd left home.

Fine. He would do it.

A grim smile tugged up the corners of his lips. "I have an idea."

CHAPTER 30

Derrick

AFTER SPLITTING up the guns between the four vehicles, hiding them as best they could, Derrick got back on the road while the rest of them stayed behind. Fourteen miles after crossing the California border he reached the California Inspection Station. Derrick scowled at the scene in front of him.

Before the crap had hit the fan, this station had been used to keep out invasive species of insects that could wreak havoc on the California agriculture industry. Drivers would be asked if they were bringing in any fruit or other items that could be carrying those species. But now that seemed less important. Even so, the inspections station was up and running.

There were seven lanes, each one leading into a covered checkpoint where inspectors could ask questions and inspect vehicles if they so chose. Derrick had been through here before. Each time at least three lanes had been opened with most of the closed lanes having an orange cone in the middle of the lane, keeping cars from entering. The remaining lanes had been blocked by enormous doors that worked like massive garage doors, making it impossible to pass.

Now though, six of the seven lanes had their doors down, completely barricading those lanes and forcing all vehicles to funnel through the one open lane. There was a lane for semi-trucks off to the right, but that had been blocked by several semis. Clearly, these people were determined to control the flow of traffic into California.

He didn't bother picking up the walkie. The range wasn't good enough to travel the miles necessary to reach the rest of his group. Especially with the mountainous terrain.

Instead, he slowly approached the open lane, his gaze skimming the men standing guard. There were three of them, all armed.

He drove forward with the ridiculous hope that they would wave him through like they had when he'd driven this way in the past.

The surly looks on their faces told him that was a distant wish.

One of the men pointed his gun—a semi-automatic rifle—directly at Derrick. Derrick drew to a stop. Forcing his body to relax, he powered down his window and smiled at the man who approached his window, his rifle slung over his shoulder. "Afternoon."

The man didn't reply, instead scanning the inside of Derrick's truck with a sharp-eyed look before resting his gaze on Derrick. "Where are you headed?"

"Sacramento." That wasn't precisely true, but what business was it of his?

"Are you transporting any weapons?"

There it was. Confirmation that Everett had been spot-on with his warning.

Derrick widened his eyes in a look of disbelief. "Well, of course. I mean, you gotta nowadays. Am I right?"

The man ignored the question, his eyes never leaving Derrick's face.

Chin-pointing at the man's rifle, Derrick smiled. "I see you're prepared."

The man gave Derrick a dirty look, like it had been a grave offense to point out that the ones taking the guns had guns of their own. "Hand over your weapon."

Not wanting to make this too easy, Derrick frowned. "You work for the government?"

The man narrowed his eyes. "Yes."

Derrick tilted his head. "Could I see some ID?"

Nostrils flaring, the man pulled out a badge and held it where Derrick could see.

Looked legit.

"Thank you."

The man glared at Derrick and held out his hand. "Your weapon."

He made a show of digging the gun out of his glove box— not his Glock, which was hidden. Instead, this was one of the guns they'd taken off of Tyson's men. Derrick handed it over. "You're giving that back, right?"

Now the man laughed as he shook his head. "No."

Derrick's mouth fell open as his head jerked back. "What? Why not?"

The man dropped the magazine, ejected the round in the chamber, then tossed the gun into a black box behind him. "No weapons are allowed to cross the border."

"Hold on. It's...it's all I've got. I mean, how am I supposed to protect myself?" He was getting into this role.

The man smirked. "That's not my problem."

"I want it back!"

The man's eyebrows shot up. "Are we going to have an issue?" He glanced at his buddy, the one who held the semi-automatic rifle. That man stepped forward, moving into position so that his rifle was only a few feet from Derrick's head.

Derrick threw his hands up like he was surrendering. "No no. I'm sorry. I just...I'm sorry." His voice broadcast fear.

Scowling, the man glanced behind Derrick. Looking in his rearview mirror, Derrick saw Matt approaching the checkpoint. Perfect timing.

The man waved Derrick through.

Acting sufficiently cowed, Derrick pulled through and drove on, not stopping until he'd gone three miles.

He just hoped the man wouldn't give Matt and his family too hard a time.

CHAPTER 31

Matt

WITH NO IDEA what had happened with Derrick except that he had made it through, Matt didn't know what to expect. Plastering a smile onto his face despite his nervousness, he pulled to a stop right where they told him to. He powered his window down. "Howdy."

A man approached his open window, his gaze less than friendly. Matt noticed a tattoo of a dragon on his right arm. Two other armed guards loitered nearby.

Dragon-man's gaze swept over Matt and his family, briefly resting on the girls in the back seat. Knowing he was probably thinking how pretty they both were made Matt's skin crawl. This was the first time he had truly been on his own— Derrick was miles ahead and Chris and Jeff were miles behind. If these men decided to do something to his family, there wouldn't be a lot he could do. He would fight to the death for his family, of course, but he desperately hoped it wouldn't come to that.

Dragon-man never cracked a smile. "Got any weapons?"

Nervous about this whole operation, Matt said, "Just two. One for me and one for my boy."

He narrowed his eyes. "Let me see them."

"What's going on, Dad?" Dylan asked, just like he was supposed to.

Matt glanced at him in the rearview mirror. "Don't know." He shifted his gaze to Dragon-man. "Why do you want to see my guns?"

Tilting his head, Dragon-man frowned deeply. "I don't want to see them. I want to have them."

The memory of the neighborhood cooperative forcing their way into his house and taking his food crashed over Matt. It had infuriated him then and this was beginning to infuriate him now. He felt himself tensing up, felt adrenaline dumping into his veins. He'd known before arriving at this inspection station that this was what was going to happen, and he'd thought he was prepared. But it turned out that having someone confiscate his guns—even ones that he'd planned on giving up—rubbed him the wrong way. Mightily.

"You can't have them," he heard himself say.

Jessica put her hand on his arm. He was supposed to give them up willingly and move along. Not make waves.

Dragon-man's eyebrows shot up. "Excuse me?"

"Matt," Jessica murmured.

Ignoring her warning, Matt scowled. "I'm sure you've heard of a little thing called the Second Amendment. You know, the one in the Bill of Rights? The one that says the people..." he tapped himself on the chest, "that would be me —have the right to keep and bear arms."

"Not anymore."

Had things changed so drastically that all of their rights had been thrown out the window at the whims of some acting governor?

Matt narrowed his eyes. "Since when?"

Dragon-man stared Matt down. "I don't have to explain anything to you. Now, hand over your weapons."

The arrogance of the man blazed a trail of indignation right through Matt. With his teeth clenched, Matt muttered, "Go to hell."

Dragon-man's eyebrows shot up, then he used his head to motion another guard over. That man pointed his semi-automatic rifle at Matt. Dragon-man narrowed his eyes at Matt. "Get. Out." He paused half a beat. "Now."

Oh crap. He should have stayed with the plan. Now he'd screwed everything up.

Still, these guys infuriated him. What if he refused to cooperate? How likely was it that the guard would shoot him in the head?

He exhaled a sigh.

It wasn't worth it to find out.

He started opening his door.

"Dad?" Kayla whispered, her voice frantic with fear.

He threw her what he hoped was a reassuring smile before stepping out of the truck. He was about the same height as Dragon-man, but not nearly as ripped. Dragon-man looked like he spent every spare moment working out. Not good. Not to mention that he and the other two guards were armed and ready, whereas Matt's guns were tucked away so as to show that he and his family were just wanting to pass through without causing a problem. Too bad he'd blown it.

Dragon-man clamped the back of Matt's neck with one

hand and wrenched him away from the open door. With the other guard's rifle trained on him, Matt wasn't about to resist. The third guard stayed a short distance away, his rifle slung low and ready.

Dragon-man marched Matt around the open door to the hood of the truck, stopping beside it with Matt facing the hood. Dragon-man held Matt there for a full second, his hand still gripping Matt's neck. Without warning, he slammed Matt face-first into the hood. Matt heard the crunch of his nose breaking at the same time that excruciating pain exploded through his head. He couldn't stop a cry of pain from climbing his throat, which was quickly clogging with blood. He heard his family screaming. The metallic taste of blood filled his mouth. He pressed his hands against the truck to gain leverage at the same time that Dragon-man yanked him upright. Blood gushed out of his nose and over his lips. He covered his face with his hands. They were immediately awash in his blood.

"Matt!" Jessica cried as she flung her door open and rushed toward him.

"Stop right there," the closest guard shouted, shifting his aim to her.

She froze, her eyes wide with terror.

Everything had gone sideways at an alarming rate. He had to put a stop to it before it got any worse. "Leave her alone!"

"Shut up," Dragon-man growled in his ear.

Forcing down his fear, Matt asked, "Do you want my guns or not?"

Dragon-man laughed. "We're gonna get your guns. And anything else we want."

Right about then would have been a great time for Jeff and

Chris to show up, but the plan was for them to appear at varying intervals—they didn't want to make it obvious that they were together. So, who knew when they would come?

Matt was on his own. And not doing so well.

"Fine," he said, as if he had a choice. "Just leave my family alone."

Dragon-man laughed. He released Matt's neck, but immediately twisted Matt's arms behind his back before securing them with a zip tie. Dragon-man shoved Matt toward the guard shack, forcing him to sit on the hard pavement. "You're gonna sit there while we search your rig."

The third guard, who'd stayed back, came over to Matt and pointed his rifle at him.

Ignoring the throbbing of his face, Matt tried to calm the fury that was coming to a boil inside him. It didn't work. Now he had an idea how Derrick had felt when Tyson's men had tied him up. Then again, they hadn't broken his nose in the process. And those had been thugs, not the government. This was all kinds of wrong.

Dragon-man walked toward the guard who was aiming his gun at Jessica. He pushed the barrel down so that it pointed at the ground, then he sauntered over to her. "Have your family get out of the truck, then unlock your RV." His voice was soft, like he was being reasonable, but Matt could see anger flashing in Jessica's eyes.

When she didn't move, he clamped a hand on her upper arm. "Now!"

That jolted her. She looked at Matt. His family was the most important thing. Not their stuff. "Do what he says, Jess."

Her jaw clenched, but she nodded before going to the truck and having the kids and Cleo get out. Cleo was growling deep in her throat. As much as Matt would have loved to see her rip out Dragon-man's throat, he knew that scenario wouldn't end well, so when Brooke kept control of Cleo with the leash, he was glad.

He watched helplessly as Dragon-man searched their truck, coming up with the two guns they'd planned on handing over anyway. No other guns were in the truck—that had been the plan.

Dragon-man handed the guns to the second guard, who dropped the magazines, emptied the chambers, and tossed the guns into a black box not far from where Matt was held captive.

Dragon-man turned to Jessica, his eyebrows raised.

She dug the keys to the RV out of her purse, then went to the RV door and unlocked it.

"All of you," Dragon-man said, looking at her and the kids, "get back in your truck."

They did as he asked. Good. Matt wanted them away from these men.

Dragon-man pulled the RV steps down, then opened the door and disappeared inside. A moment later the slide-outs rumbled open.

He was in there for a good ten minutes, and every one of those minutes had Matt's rage pounding inside his skull. This guy was searching their RV without cause and without permission. A stranger poking through their things, planning to take whatever he wanted. On behalf of the government.

Finally, after what seemed like forever, Dragon-man stepped out of the RV carrying two buckets of freeze-dried food while wearing a wide grin.

No guns though. They'd hidden those in places he hadn't looked. Yet.

That little victory helped to settle Matt.

A horn honked behind the RV.

When Matt saw Jeff getting out of his truck with a confused look, like he was wondering what the hold-up was, relief blasted through him. Not that Jeff could do a whole lot against three men with rifles at the ready, but still, he didn't feel so alone.

"This gonna take long?" Jeff asked, completely ignoring Matt, which was good. No reason to tip these guys off that they knew each other. "I got a long way to go still."

Dragon-man set the buckets of food down and walked toward Jeff. "We'll be done when we're done. Get back in your truck and wait your turn."

Jeff's gaze flicked to Matt, who knew how he must look with the blood all over his face and shirt and his hands bound behind his back. Jeff faced Dragon-man. "There a problem here?"

Dragon-man's back was to Matt, but Matt saw him tense up. "Nothing you need to worry about. Now, get back in your truck."

Matt could see Jeff look at each of the three guards in turn and could almost see the wheels turning in his head. He wanted to tell him to leave it alone, that it wasn't worth it, but he stayed quiet.

CHAPTER 32

Matt

JEFF STAYED WHERE HE WAS. Dragon-man didn't move either. He was obviously used to people following his orders the first time he gave them.

"Are you deaf, or just stupid?"

Jeff grinned, his body relaxed. "A little of both, I'm afraid."

"What?"

"Yeah," Jeff said, walking closer to Dragon-man, "drives my girlfriend crazy."

Dragon-man lifted his rifle, but by then Jeff was too close. Jeff knocked the rifle to the side. That must have caught Dragon-man off guard, because his rifle clattered to the ground. In the split-second it took Dragon-man to react, Jeff pulled his handgun out of his holster and shot him dead.

Mentally cheering, Matt looked to his left to see what the other two guards were going to do. They seemed stunned by this sudden turn of events, but it didn't take them long to recover. They both lifted their rifles and took aim, but Jeff had darted behind the back of the RV, out of their line of fire.

They marched forward in single file. The first one stepped past Matt, but when the second one moved to follow his buddy, Matt's leg shot out, tripping him. The man face-planted onto the pavement with a grunt.

A gunshot rang out to Matt's right. His head jerked in that direction. The second guard was down and not moving. Jeff had shot him from underneath the RV. Jeff popped out from under the RV and kicked the guard's rifle away, all the while pointing his gun at the third guard, who was getting to his feet.

Worried that other guards were going to show up from someplace he hadn't seen, Matt frantically looked around, but no one else appeared.

"Drop it," Jeff demanded.

The guard dropped his rifle without hesitation.

"Hands in the air," Jeff said.

The man's hands shot up.

Jeff patted him down, taking a handgun from his holster. "Sit over there."

The guard complied.

Jeff checked the other guard for a pulse. He looked at Matt, shook his head, then searched him, taking his handgun. Next, he cut the zip tie from Matt's wrists. "You okay?"

Now that he was free and the guards were neutralized, he was great. Matt jumped to his feet with a grin. "Happy to see you."

Jeff chuckled. "I'll bet." He used zip ties he found in the guard shack to bind the remaining guard's hands and feet. "I have a few questions for you," Jeff said to the guard as he squatted in front him.

Matt stood over the guard, curious to hear what Jeff was going to ask him and what the guard would say.

"Who are you working for?"

The guard leaned to the side, away from Jeff. "The state government."

"Are you saying the government is up and running in California?"

"More or less."

His vague answer rubbed Matt the wrong way. Especially after these guys had broken his nose. Matt knelt on the ground and grabbed the guard by the shirt. "What is it? More. Or less?"

The guard shrank back. "I don't know. Some of it, I guess. I mean, the government was pretty decimated by the flu, but there are enough people to keep it going. At least on a state level."

If the acting governor was taking away the rights of the people with no regard for the Constitution or the Bill of Rights, they had a real problem on their hands. Matt shook his head, then stood. "Let's go."

Jeff stood as well.

Jessica jumped out of the truck and rushed to Matt. "Are you okay?" She gently touched his face, avoiding his nose.

"I'll live." Which was the most important thing.

The kids, Cleo, and Emily joined them.

A few minutes later Chris and his family pulled up. Chris leapt from his SUV. "Looks like I missed all the fun."

"That you did," Jeff said, patting him on the shoulder.

Matt collected his two buckets of freeze-dried food,

placing them inside the RV before pulling in the slide-outs and locking the door. He came back out in time to see Chris lifting the black box partially filled with confiscated guns.

"Look what I found," Chris said with a grin.

Jeff's eyebrows shot up. "Nice haul."

Chris crammed it into the back of his SUV. "Derrick will be pleased."

"Don't forget these," Matt said, gathering up the semi-automatic rifles and putting them in the back seat of Jeff's truck.

Jeff chuckled. "Very nice."

They made a last sweep of the area to make sure they hadn't missed anything. Matt used some bottles of water from the guard shack to clean the blood from his face and hands, then he went back inside the RV to change into a clean shirt, tossing the bloodied one in the trash.

Soon, they were off with Matt in the lead.

A few miles further on, they found Derrick parked on the shoulder. He was sitting on the open gate of his truck drinking a bottle of water.

Matt parked behind him and got out.

Derrick hopped to the ground, his gaze sweeping over Matt, stopping on his swollen nose. "Oh crap." Then he noticed that Jeff and Chris were right behind Matt. "Wait. That wasn't the plan. You were all supposed to come separately." Jeff and Chris bounded up with wide smiles.

Derrick tilted his head. "What happened?"

Everyone had joined them by then. They replayed the events that Derrick had missed.

Derrick chuckled and looked at Jeff. "And... he's back."

Which Matt was more than grateful for. He didn't want to

think about what might have happened if Jeff hadn't shown up and taken out Dragon-man when he had.

Now that it was all over, he took a moment to savor the camaraderie of his friends—family, really.

Derrick stared at Matt a moment. "Not sure what we're going to do about that nose."

He wasn't either, but he didn't want to have a permanently crooked nose if he could help it.

"My aunt might be able to fix it," Emily said. "She's a nurse."

Derrick smiled. "Nice."

Matt was glad too. Otherwise he could picture Derrick or Jeff trying to straighten his nose. Not something he wanted to experience.

"By the way," Derrick said with a laugh, "you guys didn't follow my plan very well."

Matt raised his hand. "My fault." He dropped his hand to his side. "When that jerk demanded I hand over my gun, it was..." He shook his head as the memory washed over him. "It was too much."

Derrick's eyebrows rose. "Believe me. I know. I barely managed to hold myself together when he took my gun." He laughed. "It wasn't even a gun I wanted."

"That reminds me," Chris said with a twinkle in his eye. "I have a little present for you." He trotted off, coming back a few moments later carrying the black box with the confiscated guns and setting it on the ground for Derrick to see.

Derrick laughed, long and hard. "That's awesome. With all the guns we've gathered, we have enough for a small army." Then he sobered. "With the way things are going, we may actually need them."

That was Matt's fear. There were too many desperate people willing to do terrible things just to survive. Not to mention a rogue government changing all the rules.

"We have less than two hundred miles to go," Derrick added. "Let's focus on getting there in one piece."

"Amen to that," Jeff said.

They loaded into their vehicles and pulled back onto the road.

CHAPTER 33

Derrick

THICKLY WOODED forests filled Derrick's view on both sides of the Interstate. Despite the beauty of the area, he was eager to get past it and on to the farm.

They'd already passed through Truckee where not a soul had been seen, and with each mile they chewed up, he could feel their destination within reach. They'd travelled so far, surely these last miles—less than a hundred and fifty— wouldn't stop them.

They passed Donner Summit where there was still plenty of snow. Glad they would soon be in a lower elevation where it wasn't so cold, Derrick pressed on, eventually passing through Auburn.

He picked up the walkie. "Everyone doing okay? Over." He didn't want to stop until they'd arrived at the farm, but he also recognized that they had small children in their group.

"We're fine. Over." That was Matt.

"We're good. Over." Jeff.

"So far so good. Over." And Chris.

Nodding in satisfaction, Derrick scanned the road ahead. A car going their direction up ahead, but it was alone. Didn't appear to be a threat.

Before long they reached Sacramento, and when the time came, they took the Capital City Freeway, which would lead them to Highway 99 and their final destination.

As they drove south on Highway 99, drawing ever closer to the farm, Derrick felt himself relax, just a little. They had less than twenty miles to go. They were going to make it!

They passed an off-ramp. Derrick noticed two vehicles parked on the right shoulder—a beat-up blue truck and a newer Honda. He thought he saw someone in the truck, but as he passed the vehicles, it didn't look like anyone was inside after all. Still, he had an uneasy feeling.

He approached the on-ramp, but before he passed it, two police cars with lights flashing and sirens screaming came barreling down it and pulled in front of him. One of them crisscrossed the lanes in front of him, which had always meant that there was danger ahead and to slow down. But now? Now, he wasn't sure. The other police car was right in front of Derrick, moving slowly, which forced Derrick to slow.

Were the police up and running here? Had word somehow gotten to them that Derrick and his group had killed those men at the inspection station? If so, this was very, very bad. On the other hand, if these were not the actual police, that was probably worse.

The walkie squawked and Chris's voice came over the line. "We have a problem. That truck that was on the shoulder is right on my tail. And the car is on my left. Like, *right* next to me." A brief pause. "The guy does not look friendly. Over."

Derrick went from concerned to alarmed in zero seconds. If those other cars were joining in, it seemed much less likely that these police cars held actual police officers. He picked up the walkie. "There are two police cars in front of me that won't let me pass, but I don't think it's the legit police." He released the talk button as a million scenarios flashed through his mind, none of them good. He pressed Talk again. "The next exit is ours. We'll take it and see what happens. Over."

As they approached their exit, a third police car, which had been parked on the left shoulder, joined the other two, coming up close to Derrick's left side.

A car to his left, two cars in front, and two in the back.

They were being herded.

That's when he saw a blockade of cars and trucks stretched out across the highway up ahead. They had no choice but to take the off-ramp they'd planned on taking anyway.

Frantically trying to figure out how to get away, he briefly considered opening fire. But a firefight would end with casualties, including many from their group. If he'd been on his own it would have been a different story, but he cared about his people. More deeply than he ever thought he would. Plus, they had women and children with them. No. He couldn't risk a gunfight. Not when they were surrounded by five cars full of bad guys.

With nowhere to go but where the police cars were leading them, Derrick felt a sense of helplessness that he hadn't experienced since leaving home.

Another car joined the parade, coming up on Derrick's right. Then another. They were boxed in.

He took the exit. The rest of their group followed. They

were funneled into the parking lot of a large post office where all seven cars surrounded them. Armed men—at least two per car--and even a couple of women, got out of the cars, their weapons pointed at Derrick and their group.

A man who had been driving one of the police cars—not wearing a uniform, Derrick noted—leaned inside the police car, and when he stood, he spoke into the car's public address system, his voice loud and clear. "Everyone out of their vehicles. Keep your hands where I can see them."

Exhaling audibly, Derrick picked up the walkie. "Do what he says. Over."

"Or we can take them out," Jeff said. "Over."

"No," Chris said. "I have children in my car. Not worth the risk. Over."

Derrick pressed the talk button. "I agree. Over."

"Now!" Pretend-cop said.

Reminding himself to relax his jaw, Derrick slid his Glock under his seat and stepped out with his hands in the air. He looked down the line at the others in his group. They were doing the same. Brooke had hold of Cleo's leash.

Men swarmed them, patting them down, taking any weapons they found and emptying their pockets.

Someone hit the backs of Derrick's legs, making him fall to his knees.

"Hands on your head!"

Seething with anger, he complied.

He looked at the others in their group. Nearly everyone was on their knees with their hands on their heads in a long row. The only exceptions were Amy and Paisley. They were comforting their children who were crying hysterically.

Pretend-cop walked over to them, his eyes sharp and his

hands clasped behind his back. He walked the length of them, then turned around and started walking back, pausing in front of Kayla, Brooke, Jessica, and Emily, his gaze sliding over each of them slowly. With a grin, he moved on, stopping in front of Matt. "What happened to you?"

Derrick glanced Matt's way. His nose was obviously broken.

Matt stared straight ahead, his jaw clenched.

Pretend-cop grinned and strolled on down the line in Derrick's direction. He wore jeans and a t-shirt, and on his head he wore a ball cap turned backwards. Tattoos snaked up both arms. He looked like a gang-banger, as did all the people in his crew. Most likely that's exactly what they were, which made Derrick wonder if they should have stayed in their own neighborhood despite it being taken over by a gang.

Had they driven hundreds of miles just to be faced with another gang?

He shook his head.

Pretend-cop noticed. He stomped over to Derrick, stopping in front of him. "Got a problem?"

Defiance slammed through Derrick. He stared at the man. "Who are you and what do you want?"

Pretend-cop smiled, then stood straighter and puffed out his chest. "We're the Emperors. As in Emperors of the New World." His leaned over slightly and stared right at Derrick. "You can call me Emperor Randy."

Biting back a response that he knew would get him beat, if not outright shot, Derrick stared back.

Randy straightened.

"Don't tell me," Derrick said, not able to hold back the sarcasm, "you want us to pay a tax."

Randy smiled. "A tax. Yes, let's call it that." He turned to his crew. "Hear that? You're tax collectors now."

Chuckles all around.

Derrick wanted to get this over with and get to the farm. They were so close now. He wouldn't make the same mistakes he'd made with Tyson. "How much is your tax?"

Randy tapped his chin like he was thinking it over, then he grinned. "I'm just teasing. I know exactly how much my tax is." He paused dramatically. "Fifty percent."

He wanted *half* of their food? That was outrageous.

Maybe he could be reasoned with. Or maybe fifty percent was the start of his negotiation.

Using all of his self-control to keep the disgust out of his voice, Derrick said, "We can't spare that much. As you see, we have a large group."

Randy's lips tilted up in a wide smile. "What makes you think I care about that?" His smile vanished. "I don't. All I care about is taking care of my people. And you are not my people."

This guy was an idiot. Derrick suppressed a laugh. "Wait. I thought you were the Emperor. Doesn't that make everyone your people? Including us?"

One of Randy's men snickered. Randy glared at the man. The snicker shut off like someone had hit a switch. Randy turned back to Derrick. "Are you trying to be funny?" At the look of embarrassed fury on Randy's face, Derrick couldn't stop his lips from twitching, which seemed to enrage Randy all the more. "You need to learn to show some respect." Randy's gaze flicked to one of his men. Derrick barely had a chance to brace himself before the butt of a rifle slammed into his back right between his shoulder blades. He jerked forward, but managed to throw his hands out just in time to keep from smashing his face into the pavement.

Gasps came from his group. Straightening, he put his hands back on his head and looked at Randy as rage tore through him like a living thing.

Randy grinned at Derrick, then his gaze swept over the trucks Derrick and the others had been driving. His eyes went to each member of their group. "You will all pay a tax of fifty percent. Only then will I allow you to leave."

Fuming with resentment at the audacity of Randy and his crew, Derrick felt his entire body go rigid. Trying to calm himself, he focused on the men and women who were with Randy. Fourteen in all and not one showed a hint of discipline. Some slouched, others closed their eyes as they rolled their shoulders, still others were quietly chatting instead of being on alert.

Amateurs. Every last one of them.

Even so, they outnumbered Derrick's group and all of them were armed.

CHAPTER 34

Matt

MATT WAS ABOUT to tell *Emperor Randy* where he could put his tax when the throbbing in his nose reminded him that he didn't want to get beat down if he could avoid it. Instead, he consoled himself with the fact that they were almost to the farm. They could regroup there.

Randy looked them all over. "No objections? Good." He motioned for one of his men to join him. The man did, holding out his hands, which held the keys they'd taken from the pockets of Matt and the other drivers. He picked up one set and held them up. "Whose are these?"

"Mine," Chris said.

"You're the SUV?"

Chris nodded. "Yeah."

Randy handed the keys to his aid, who set them on the ground in front of Chris.

Randy held up another set. "And these?"

Matt recognized his keys. He would be glad to get them back. "Those are mine."

"Ah. You're the RV."

"Yeah."

Randy examined Matt's keys, then walked over to stand in front of Matt. "Are the keys to the RV on here?"

The guy wanted to get in the RV and take some food. Fine. Matt wouldn't fight over that. He just wanted to get his family safely away. "No."

Randy smiled at him. "Where are the keys to the RV?"

"In my truck."

Still smiling, Randy said, "Get them."

Matt dropped his hands to his sides and stood, aware that one of Randy's men was right behind him with his gun pointed at Matt. He opened the door to his truck and reached into the little compartment where he kept the RV keys and took them out, then walked over to Randy, who had his hand out. Feeling that familiar fury building inside him, the one that stemmed from people taking what was his when they had no right, he gritted his teeth as he set the keys in Randy's open palm.

Randy pocketed the truck keys as well as the RV keys. "Thank you." His smile vanished. "Back on your knees."

Nostrils flaring, Matt complied.

Randy held up another set.

"Mine," Jeff said, his voice filled with irritation.

"You're the truck with the trailer."

"Yep."

After walking over to Jeff, Randy stood in front of him as he examined the ring of keys before holding one up. "This is for the trailer?"

"Yep."

He smiled. "Excellent." Randy pocketed Jeff's keys, then walked over to Derrick. "And you're the lead truck?" When Derrick nodded, his face set in grim determination, Randy dropped the last set of keys on the ground in front of him. Wearing a self-satisfied grin, Randy turned to face all of them. "Your tax has been paid. You may leave."

Confused, Matt got to his feet. "I need my keys."

Laughter burst from Randy's mouth. "Keys to what? That truck and RV belong to me now." He tilted his head. "That paid the tax. Well, part of it."

A buzzing began in Matt's head as his fury began to boil over. It felt as if steam was actually escaping out of his ears. His hands curled into fists.

"Matt," Jessica said in a warning voice.

Derrick stepped forward, effectively blocking Matt from approaching Randy. "What do you mean it paid part of it?"

Randy shrugged. "The other truck and trailer paid the rest."

"What?" Jeff roared, then he rushed toward Randy.

Two of Randy's men stepped in Jeff's path as Randy stumbled backward. Jeff barreled through the men, but when a bullet hit the ground by Jeff's feet, he stopped.

"I'd prefer not to shoot you," Randy said, "but I will if I have to."

"Leave it, Jeff," Emily said beside him, her voice urgent.

"Listen to your wife," Randy said with a sneer.

Matt almost expected Jeff to say she was his girlfriend, not his wife, but Jeff just glared at Randy, his face a mask of rage.

"Now," Randy said, his voice calm, "get in your remaining vehicles and leave before we get mean."

"Wait," Jessica said.

Matt turned to her with a look of surprise. What was she doing? It was time to go.

Randy turned to Jessica with a look of annoyance. "What?"

"Can we at least get some of our things? Clothes and personal items? Please...Emperor Randy?"

The use of his fake name seemed to delight him. He smiled at her as he took a step toward her, which alarmed Matt. He stepped in front of her. The smile vanished from Randy's lips. "Move."

Matt didn't budge until a pair of hands roughly yanked him away.

"Now," Randy said to Jessica, "why don't you and I go into your RV and you can get a few things." He narrowed his eyes at Matt. "You stay here."

Matt didn't know how much more of this he could take, but two of Randy's men had their guns trained on him. Jeff and Derrick had a pair of men on them as well. Chris stood with his family along with Paisley and Serena. With two women and three small children to keep safe, there wasn't much he could do. Matt glanced at Dylan and the girls. Dylan met his gaze. Anger burned in his eyes. Matt gave an imperceptible shake of his head.

Randy grabbed Jessica's arm and began walking toward the RV.

Matt couldn't stop himself. "Wait!"

Everyone turned and looked at him, including Randy, who released Jessica's arm and strode back to Matt. "What is it now?"

The thought of this evil low-life being alone with his wife made Matt's gut churn. "Let me get the things from the RV."

Randy stared at him, which was when Matt noticed how empty his eyes looked. Like he had no soul.

A smile spread across Randy's face. "I have a better idea." He shifted his gaze to Brooke and Kayla. He studied them for several seconds before turning back to Matt. "How about we make a trade? You get to keep your rig and I..." His smile grew. "I get to keep one of your daughters."

It was as if Matt had been slammed in the gut by a two by four. "No!"

One of Randy's eyebrows cocked. "Maybe I'll keep the rig and both of the girls." He licked his lips as he slowly nodded.

Adrenaline flooded Matt's veins. His hands curled into fists as pounding filled his ears. Now that the fuse of his rage had been lit, he couldn't have stopped himself if he'd wanted to. His face must have broadcast his intent, because before he could follow through on his heart's deepest desire, Randy pulled a gun out of his waistband and pressed it to Matt's skull.

"I wouldn't do that if I was you." His voice was low and deadly and his eyes glittered with malice.

Matt felt no fear for himself. Not a single drop. His thoughts were completely focused on his family. He would die for them. No question. With his jaw clenched so hard it began to ache, and with his eyes boring into Randy's, he said, "If you or your men touch either one of my daughters, I will rip your head off."

Randy's eyebrows shot up and his eyes widened like he was stunned Matt had the guts to say that. "I don't think you're in much of a position to make demands." He glanced at the gun pressed to Matt's forehead. "In case you hadn't noticed, I could blow your head off with a twitch of my finger." Unexpectedly, Randy smiled and pulled the gun away from Matt's head, tucking it in his waistband. "Just to show you that I'm an Emperor who cares about his people, I'll let you live. And..." his smile widened, "I won't take your girls. But you'd better adjust that attitude."

Relief crashed over Matt, but he managed to keep his expression neutral.

Randy turned his back on Matt, but Randy's men were still right there, their guns trained on him.

Randy strode back to Jessica, who looked like she wasn't sure if she wanted to kill Matt or kiss him. Then, without another word, Randy walked past her and to the RV, stopping beside the door.

CHAPTER 35

Jessica

SWALLOWING over the giant knot in her throat, Jessica stared at Matt. The way he'd confronted this maniac, clearly he'd lost his mind for a minute there. But she loved him all the more for doing it. He'd proven beyond a shadow of a doubt that he would fiercely protect his family. And really, if that monster hurt any of her children, she would be happy to kill the man herself.

"Woman!" Randy shouted.

Startled, Jessica spun around and looked at him. He was standing beside the door to the RV, waiting for her. The way he'd called her by her gender only emphasized the disdain he had for women. And the threat to take one of her daughters? He was despicable.

She didn't want to go in the RV with him now. She had been stupid to call attention to herself and prolong this ordeal.

She pushed a smile onto her lips. "Never mind. I...I don't need anything after all."

Randy tilted his head. "Come here." His voice was soft and menacing. "Now."

Oh no, oh no, oh no. She shifted her gaze to Matt, who looked like he wanted to kill every last one of these guys.

As much as she wanted Matt to do something, she also knew that if he stepped up, Randy would hurt him, maybe even kill him. Watching the man at the border slam Matt's face into the hood of the truck had been horrifying. The thought of anything else happening to him made her stomach churn.

No. She'd brought this on herself and she would have to see it through.

With her heart thumping painfully, she forced herself to walk toward Randy, stopping several feet away.

He handed her the key. "Open it."

What was he going to do when they were alone?

Dizzy with fear, she unlocked the door to the RV and pulled down the steps. On shaky legs, she climbed the steps—one, two, three—and stepped inside.

The familiarity of the interior served to calm her. She and Matt and the kids had made so many good memories in here over the years, but this would be the last time she would step foot inside. All because this monster was taking it from them. *Stealing* it. He had no right.

He climbed in behind her. "Nice place."

The stink of him surrounded her—body odor and bad breath—making her want to retch.

She wanted to turn around and shove him out the door. Maybe he'd fall on his head and crack open his skull. Spill his brains all over the pavement. The thought brought a smile to her lips.

"Never been inside one of these before," he said.

Great. He'd probably break everything.

Thankful her fear had been replaced with anger, she pressed the buttons to open the slide-outs so that she could get the items she wanted, aware that Randy was watching her every move. To learn how to use the RV or for other reasons, she didn't know and didn't want to know.

First, she took a photo album out of a cabinet and set it on the counter. Then, she went into the bedroom and found the necklace her mother had given her, clasping it around her neck. Next, she gathered some of her and Matt's clothes—she didn't have a suitcase to put them in as they always took the clothes directly from their closets at home and hung them in the RV closet, so she stuffed them in paper bags from the pantry. Then, when Randy was busy exploring, she slipped several envelopes of freeze-dried food into the bags as well. Finally, she grabbed the kids' suitcases and wheeled them to the door.

Randy followed her. Barely able to stand the sight of him, she forced herself to meet his stare. "That's it."

He grinned in that way that made her wish she had the skills to wipe the smile off of his face.

Beyond grateful that he hadn't touched her, she carried everything outside and set it all on the ground. When everything was outside, Randy came down the stairs and held out his hand. She stared at his hand before taking the RV keys out of her pocket and placing them in his palm.

These were Matt's keys. She still had her own set in her purse, but she kept that information to herself.

He grinned. "Thank you."

She didn't reply.

He waved her away like she was a pesky insect. "Get back in line."

Burning with anger, she hurried over to Matt, who folded her into his arms. She sagged against him as tears welled up.

Randy went back inside the RV and pulled the slide-outs back in before coming out, closing the door, and folding up the stairs. He walked past them, then looked at his crew before making a twirling motion with his finger. At that, they all got in their cars, with one man getting in Jeff's truck and another getting in their truck.

Bristling at seeing strangers—criminals—acting like the truck and RV was theirs, Jessica felt her whole body tense. She knew Jeff and Emily had to feel exactly the same, and when she looked at Jeff, she saw his hands clenching and unclenching, and his lips pulled back, baring his teeth.

Despite how Jessica and her group felt, Randy and his men drove away, leaving Jessica and her family and friends standing in the parking lot in a helpless rage.

"I'm gonna kill that SOB," Jeff muttered.

Jessica had no doubt he meant it.

"Okay," Derrick said, "gather round."

Glad he was once again taking the lead, and with her hand clasped in Matt's, Jessica stepped closer to Derrick.

He looked at each of them in turn. "I know how angry you are. I feel exactly the same way. But we're almost to the farm. It's literally, like, ten miles away. Let's just get there." He glanced at Emily. "We have no idea what we'll find. So, for now, let's focus on that." Derrick looked at Jessica and Matt. "Let's put your stuff in the back of my truck." He smiled grimly. "Then we'll cram everyone into my truck and just get there. Okay?"

Heads nodded all around.

"You know," Chris said, "that idiot never searched my SUV." A smile grew on his face. "We have that whole bucket of confiscated guns in there."

"Nice," Derrick said as his eyes lit up. "I'd forgotten about that."

Having a bucket of guns was great, but it didn't exactly make up for losing her home on wheels.

Then she remembered what she'd managed to take. Smiling at the small victory, she said, "I took some freeze-dried food."

Everyone looked at her with surprise, but Matt didn't look impressed. Instead, he looked angry. "That was a big risk. What if he'd caught you?"

Annoyed that he hadn't praised her courage, when she considered the seriousness of what could have happened, her shoulders slumped. "You're right. It was dumb."

He smiled softly. "No. It was very brave." Then he kissed her.

The feeling of triumph returned. "Thank you."

Her mood brighter, she helped get everything loaded into the bed of Derrick's truck, then the kids and Cleo climbed inside the cab while Jessica, Matt, Jeff, and Emily got in the bed. There was room for one in Chris's SUV, but the four of them decided to all sit together in the bed of Derrick's truck.

Once they were all settled, they drove out of the parking lot.

CHAPTER 36

Matt

EVERY TIME he pictured Randy driving off with everything he and his family had left in the world—except the few items Jessica had managed to salvage—Matt found it hard to think of anything but his anger. Then he looked at Jessica, who smiled softly at him. He twisted around and saw his three children sitting safely inside Derrick's truck.

Warmth and calm spread over him. Yes, he'd lost his truck and RV, which infuriated him, but in reality he had everything that was truly important to him. His family, who he loved more than life itself. That was all that mattered.

Slipping his hand into Jessica's, when she gently squeezed his hand, he squeezed back.

They rode in silence until Emily shouted, "There it is."

They turned down an unpaved road that led to a moderately-sized house. It wasn't as large as their house had been in Utah. Still, it looked roomy enough. Anyway, it wasn't like they had anywhere else to go. They would make do. Assuming Emily's aunt and uncle even took them in.

As they drew closer, Matt scanned the surrounding area. It wasn't exactly the idyllic image he'd envisioned, but it was still nice. There was a sizable garden off to the side of the house and a huge pasture with several cows milling about. A wide river flowed a distance behind the house. A source of water. Perfect.

The moment they stopped in front of the house, Emily climbed out of the bed of the truck and raced to the front door.

"Em!" Jeff called out. "Hold up. You don't know if it's safe."

Her hand poised to knock, she stopped and looked at him, then dropped her hand to her side.

Matt noted that there was no red X painted on the door, so that was a good sign. And it didn't smell like rotting corpses. Another good sign. But what if someone had taken over their farm, killing her aunt and uncle in the process? What if they weren't there at all?

Jeff hopped out of the bed of the truck, as did Matt and Jessica. Derrick joined them as they faced the porch. If they knocked on that door and her aunt and uncle didn't answer...

Had they come all this way, gone through all that turmoil, lost everything, for nothing?

Uncertainty was thick in the air.

The front door swung open and a couple stood in the doorway. They looked like they were in their late fifties. Covering her mouth with one hand, the woman stared at Emily. "Is it really you?"

"Hello, Aunt Sarah."

Sarah threw her arms around Emily and they clung to each other for an extended hug.

Emily turned to her uncle. "Uncle Frank. It's so good to see you." A wide smile broke across his face as he hugged her too.

So, they were there. A smile slowly grew on Matt's mouth.

By then, everyone was out of both the truck and the SUV, although they hung back.

Frank looked over Emily's shoulder at the assembled group, his forehead creasing with concern. "Who are all these people?"

Jeff joined Emily on the porch.

"You know Jeff, of course."

Frank shook Jeff's hand before Sarah drew him in for a hug. "So good to see you," Sarah said with a warm smile.

"These people," Emily said, sweeping her hand out to encompass their entire group, "are basically my family."

Frank's eyebrows shot up. "Oh?"

Emily laughed. "Yes. We've travelled together all the way from Utah." She sighed deeply. "It's been a rough trip. But we made it." She turned and looked at the group before facing her aunt and uncle. "I kind of promised them that you would, well, that you would let them stay."

Frank's eyebrows rose even higher. "You did, did you?"

"I'm sorry. We had nowhere else to go."

Frank's eyebrows settled into their normal position as he slowly studied each member of their group.

Matt was certain her uncle must be overwhelmed. There were eight adults, three teenagers, three little children, and one dog. That was a lot of mouths to feed.

Derrick stepped forward. "Mr. Miller, I'm Derrick Weathers."

Frank shook his hand. "Call me Frank."

Derrick nodded. "We understand if you need time to decide if we should be allowed to stay, but I can promise you that we will carry our weight. We will tackle any job that you assign us. And if you do decide to let us stay, we will be forever grateful." He paused. "On the other hand, if you decide to turn us away, we'll understand and we won't hold it against you."

"Frank," Jeff said. "These people have had our backs on so many occasions. They're like family to Emily and me. They truly are."

Frank looked from Jeff to Emily to the assembled group and then to his wife, who tentatively smiled.

"I'm not promising anything, but we could use a few extra hands around here," Frank said, his voice gruff. "There's lots to do." He paused. "I know we can count on Jeff for security. Are any of you capable in that regard?"

Matt held back a chuckle.

"They are, Frank," Jeff said.

A small smile tugged at Frank's lips, then he sobered. "Our food stores are getting low. What do you have?"

"We have some," Jeff said. "But we had a whole lot more before, well, before the rest was taken." He exhaled loudly. "Just a few miles from here, as a matter of fact."

Frank's eyes widened. "Don't tell me. It was those Emperors, wasn't it?"

So, they'd been causing trouble in the whole area. Why didn't that surprise Matt? The fury Matt had managed to suppress since leaving the post office parking lot came roaring back.

"What do you know about them?" Jeff asked.

Frank shook his head, his expression darkening. "They're becoming a thorn in the side of honest, hard-working people all over."

Jeff frowned deeply. "They took my truck and trailer as well as Matt and Jessica's truck and RV."

Frank shook his head, clearly disturbed by this news. "Well, why don't you all come around back to the patio and we can get to know each other."

Sarah nodded. "I have some fresh baked loaves of bread cooling." She motioned for everyone to enter. "I'm sure you're hungry."

"Thank you, Aunt Sarah," Emily said.

The thought of eating fresh bread made Matt's mouth water, and he eagerly followed everyone around back where they settled into chairs or along the low garden wall that lined the covered patio.

"I like it here," Jessica whispered from beside him.

He did too. They'd only just arrived, but the feeling he got was one of home. They would have to prove to Frank and Sarah that it was worth having them there, but Matt had every intention of showing them that they would be an asset to their farm.

He looked at the others as they chatted excitedly, obviously relieved to have finally reached their destination. These were his people, his tribe, his family, and he would work hard to make this place a home for them, a place where they would feel safe and where they would thrive. But the best thing was, he knew they would work just as hard, because that's the kind of people they were. Together they would create a safe haven where they would make a life for themselves, because despite the fact that this new world had gone mad, they still carried hope that life could be good again. It was up to them to make it happen. And they would.

———

Thank you for reading Forced Exodus. The next book in the series is No Safe Place and is available now.

ABOUT THE AUTHOR

Christine has always loved to read, but enjoys writing suspenseful novels as well. She has her own eReader and is not embarrassed to admit that she is a book hoarder. One of Christine's favorite activities is to go camping with her family and read, read, read while enjoying the beauty of nature.

I love to hear from my readers. You can contact me in any of the following ways:
www.christinekersey.com
christine@christinekersey.com

Made in the USA
Coppell, TX
12 February 2022